the shattered Fabergé Egg

Advantage™ FICTION

T. T. Johnson

The Shattered Faberge Egg by T.T. Johnson
Copyright © 2014 by T.T. Johnson
All Rights Reserved.
ISBN: 978-1-59755-359-9
Published by: ADVANTAGE BOOKS™
                Longwood, Florida, USA
                www.advbookstore.com

This book and parts thereof may not be reproduced in any form, stored in a retrieval system or transmitted in any form by any means (electronic, mechanical, photocopy, recording or otherwise) without prior written permission of the author, except as provided by United States of America copyright law.

The Faberge Egg …A Novel is a work of fiction. Names, characters, places and incidents either are a product of the author's imagination and are not to be construed as real, or are used fictitiously. Any resemblance to actual persons (living or dead), businesses, companies, events, locales or settings is entirely incidental.

First Printing: March 2014
14 15 16 17 18 19 20   10 9 8 7 6 5 4 3 2 1
Printed in the United States of America

The Shattered Faberge Egg

Cast of Characters

Kate Stenson Burnett Harper	Kate
Kenneth Chase Burnett	Kate's husband
Emma Burnett	Kate and Ken's daughter
Logan Burnett	Kate and Ken's adopted son
Forrest Burnett	Ken's father
Maureen Burnett	Ken's mother
Robert Burnett	Ken's brother
Evelyn Burnett (Aunt Evie, Aunt Evil)	Forrest's aunt, family matriarch
Charles Stenson	Kate's father
Suzanne (Mimi) Stenson	Kate's mother
Jill & Travis Matteson	Kate's sister and brother-in-law
Shelby & Sam Matteson	Travis & Jill's twins
Mark & Maggie Johnson	Friends w/ Kate & Ken
Belinda Brunson	Friend of Kate
Joanne Taylor	Kate's best friend (childhood)
Jackson (Jax) Harper	Current husband, earlier boyfriend

T.T. Johnson

Chapter 1

There are parts of Mammoth Cave that are pitch black dark, absolute and total darkness. The tour guide asked us to turn off all flashlights for a few seconds to experience complete darkness. I began getting anxious and was remembering my life when it was just like being in a dark cave and was frightened; blinded by darkness and sometimes squeezed into tight spots.

At that moment, in the depths of my consciousness, my mind drifted to being punched awake at 3 am. He was very agitated and I woke up to him punching me in the head. He punched my ear while standing beside the bed. Pain seared through my head and I was disoriented because I was not fully awake. I tried to roll out of the way but he was faster than me. He delivered another blow hitting me in the nose. My nose began to bleed and tears ran down my face responding to the pain of the blows.

I covered my face with my hands for protection scrambling out of the bed to my feet. It was dark and the blood was starting to drip from my nose. I braced myself for his next punch but he slapped me instead and I was very scared. Attacking me in my sleep was so vicious.

"Stop it, stop it." I screamed.

I thought I had to get out of here. He might try to kill me one day. I wished someone would have warned me what I was getting into.

My emotions were all over the place and I was tired of walking on eggshells, trying so hard not to make a sound by cracking one. I never knew what would set him off and I was always living in fear. I had trouble sleeping.

I despised myself for closing my eyes and allowing it to happen again. I refused to fight back. How could I? How could I hit him? I began to minimize how bad the attacks were and told myself, "This one was not bad." It would prepare me for what the day would bring. The mental pain was difficult to bear. My thoughts about what he was doing felt worse than the actual blows, kicks or scratches to my skin. I was injured mentally more than physically.

The damage to my personal belongings: clothing, furniture, and pictures seemed like cruel punishment and caused me more agony. I wondered what I did to cause someone to lash out at me in such a brutal manner and I wanted it to stop. But I could not fight back. I didn't know what to do or who to reach out to. If I did say something the consequences would be too devastating. So in a way I was punishing myself for something that wasn't my fault.

Who would believe this was happening to me? I wanted to protect him but he hurt me over and over. This assault lasted longer than the last one and I was struggling day to day with my feelings of anger. I had been angry at him so long that my anger had turned inward - almost to depression. Uncontrollably, I could not escape the grips of self-doubt. Why me? Am I ever going to live a normal life again? Did I do something to deserve this? Was this my fault?

Springtime is a beautiful time of year and I love it; an expression of how life can begin again after a long, colorless season. Watching winter turning into spring and azaleas beginning to bloom is like life bursting forth all around.

I am a North Carolina girl through and through. I was born into a Southern family in Asheville and raised in a country club environment. My father, Charles Stenson, worked hard as an attorney to provide a comfortable life for my older sister, Jill, and me. I still remember him coming home after a long day, giving me a hug, and appreciating the beauty of the outdoors. "Kate, always remember where you came from."

At the time, I didn't understand what my father meant. It wasn't until many years later that his words would find meaning in my life. He meant the family you come from made the person you came to be.

My father's work ethic was "finish your work and do a better job than expected." He believed that it was vital for him to work hard, do a good job, and leave things better than he found them.

The Shattered Faberge Egg

I remember when I was eleven and my sister Jill was thirteen, we began to work at the law office during the summers. None of our friends had to work, but Daddy thought it was important to instill within us his work ethic. The pay was hourly and we received payroll checks that we had to cash. This helped teach us the value of money at an early age and we learned lessons that stayed with us.

One summer, Jill and I started working by doing the filing. We had to take the paperwork for nearly one hundred clients and put it into their files in the law firm's gigantic filing room. We worked in the conference room, which is where the office staff had put all the paperwork that needed filing. Jill and I were supposed to "file the pile," one client at a time. "Pile of poo" was what Jill called it. We giggled and began the dreaded task that seemed impossible to two young girls.

The stacks of papers were large, and huge paperclips on them made it hard to stack them without the papers beginning to slide, so Jill and I decided to take off all the paperclips and then begin to file. The office manager nearly had a stroke when she discovered what we had done—she had already been worried that we would spill soda on them. She ran to my dad and almost pulled off his suit coat dragging him down the hall to the conference room to show him our mess. I know she was thinking, "You spoiled little brats! Look at what you have done!"

Dad never said a word to the office manager, but instead spoke directly to us. "Fix this," he said, "then finish up the filing that you started and do a good job." It took us several days to reorganize the files, but we got every paperclip back in place and put each file where it needed to go. Because of the mess we had made, we wound up working longer that summer than Daddy had intended. But we made him proud.

The time clock was right outside the bookkeeper's office and it made a loud punch sound when you pushed in your time card. Jill and I would often clock in or out for each other until our dad put a stop to it. He said that in real life no one could punch your time card for you.

Daddy took us to lunch on the days we worked and he always introduced us as his beautiful daughters, Jill and Kate. This kind of introduction made us feel proud to be a part of our family. He taught us to speak up and be heard and look people right in the eye. He expected us to call people by name.

When Daddy gave us instructions, he only told us once. Out of respect for him, we never questioned him or even considered not doing what he had asked. Daddy never yelled at us, because not wanting to disappoint him was enough to keep us in line.

When Daddy was angry with me, he would say, "Kate. I love you, but I am disappointed." This was far worse than a spanking or any other kind of discipline. I was so happy to finish the job that summer and I bought Top Siders with the money I had earned filing at the firm.

The fresh smell of brewing coffee jolted me out of my memories of Daddy and the office.

It is peaceful this morning on the patio. I hear Jax in the kitchen making coffee. He likes it stronger than I do, but then he is stronger than I am so it makes sense. I love my husband, Jackson Lee Harper, and cannot imagine life without him. He is self-confident, alert, and very accomplished in his career as a news photographer. He's not a mountain boy, but that's OK. I love to watch him surf…it makes me fall in love with him all over again. He was surfing the Texas coast by Galveston growing up or near Surf City pier on the coast of North Carolina. Jax has surfed all over taking his board on photo shoots as well.

"How's my lil' Nugget? How about some coffee? Just for you I made it a little less intense." I roll my eyes and laugh while he gives me a hug and pats my behind. "I need to run to Home Depot so I'm going to get ready and go."

No man has ever loved me as Jax does. We live in peace most of the time unless he does something to irritate me. Then I flame up and 30 seconds later, we are laughing as we move on. I live in the realm of "eat my pixie dust and have a super sparkly day."

I enjoyed relaxing on the chaise lounge and looking at the sunshine on a beautiful day. Who would have thought that just a few years ago this kind of relaxation was impossible for me? Back then my life was filled with dread, fear and loathing all at once. My life was like a Faberge Egg shining and beautiful on the outside but when you opened the egg the inside of the shell was held together with duct tape, band aids and super glue. My life was broken to pieces but now it is glued back together with Jax mending the hairline cracks and Emma as the band aid and Jill was the duct tape keeping everything in place.

Suddenly my cell rang. It's Jill. The relationship I have with my sister is much deeper than a typical sibling bond. Jill is a rock of stability and she has always been there for me, no matter what. We are close friends and confidants, and I can tell her anything. During the darkest times of my past, I could always sense the glimmering light of my sister standing by me, wanting to do more to help, but respecting my boundaries. Where would I be without you, Jill?

"Hey there, Jill. What's up?"

"Travis and I are thinking about going to Keeneland in Lexington in April. Do you and Jax want to go?"

"Yes, of course I want to go, I have never been to the horse races in Keeneland."

"I've already texted Emma, so we have a plan to visit Sam and Shelby at UK then to the races. Then we could go back to Mammoth Cave if you like." Jill said.

"That's not even funny let me call you back." I said.

Sam and Shelby (Travis and Jill's twins) are in school at the University of Kentucky and we visited them last year and as a family we went to Mammoth cave. I was so excited to peek inside the longest cave system in the world and had heard about the cool air that was inside the beautiful rock cave.

When we arrived, I found out a tour is actually a hike inside the earth 200 to 300 feet below the surface.

I told Jill that I expected to walk in with my Starbucks and peek at the cave over a rail and then bolt on out of the cave. Jill had already paid for the whole group to go on a tour.

Jax pulled out a LED headlight headband from his backpack because the warning sign said no backpacks, no purses and no packages. Jax was always prepared and used situational awareness as his motto.

Jill stated, "You wanted to do a tour and they are two hours long. Get ready to squeeze into some tight spaces within the cold damp cave." Jill smiled knowing I was about to flip out.

"I did not even bring a coat because I did not have one that matched this outfit."

We climbed down a long stair case and I noticed the sparkle on the walls and the floor and mentioned how much I liked it. The tour guide said it is the gypsum which contains calcium sulfate.

Shelby said, "Only Aunt Kate would notice sparkles."

I asked Emma, Sam and Shelby, "Which one of you thought taking Aunt Kate caving was a good idea?"

The guide hiked us past stalagmites and into the Rotunda Room and told us that Mammoth Cave was home to the endangered eyeless cave shrimp which is a sightless albino shrimp. I was once like a cave shrimp, not seeing what was going on around me. How could I have not known? I whispered to Jill you are about to be endangered if you don't get me out of this darn cave. It was chilly 55 degrees inside and very dark. I hung onto Jax' beltloop because I wanted to be near the light on his head.

We listened as the tour guide explained the eroded sandstone in the Frozen Niagara Room and the Cedar Sink which is a massive sinkhole with a small river entering it. He told us about Fat Man's Misery a passageway that has been smoothed and polished for years by "spelunkers" and finally about Bottomless Pit which drops 105 feet deep. I had been "spelunking" through life for years could not believe I had volunteered to do it again inside this truly amazing and very unique cave. The guide said caves were nature's final frontier.

I said, "Hey James T. Kirk how much longer?" Jill elbowed me meaning stop talking.

My IPhone alerts me that Emma sent a tweet. The chirp brought me back to the present. Emma's tweet appears at the top of my phone screen. *Going to Keeneland horse races in April #turnup #swag*

After taking the chicken out of the oven I dialed Jill's cell again.

The Shattered Faberge Egg

"I see you and Emma already made plans for us to go to Lexington to Keeneland. According to Emma's Twitter post we are going in April."

"That's funny. It will be great to have the family together again." Jill said.

"Emma is upset with me because I was following her friends on Twitter and Instagram. I liked a few of her friend's pictures on Instagram and she said that was social suicide for her. Emma said, Mom, that is so embarrassing, and pleaded with me to unfollow them."

Jill was sympathetic with me and said teenage girls were challenging and that Shelby was like that at that age.

I said, "Just last week I went to pick Emma up at a friend's house and could not find her."

I texted her... *Where are you? I am looking for you.*

Emma texted back... *I am forking in the yard.*

Auto correct on her IPhone changed it to...*I am f-ing in the yard.*

She quickly texted back... *fork, fork, forking a yard. So sorry Mommy."*

Jill laughed, "What is forking a yard?" I explained that about 5 kids line up each with a box of white plastic forks and place the forks tines down in the yard and make rows of white picket fences and then the only way to remove the forks was by hand. Jill said, "We just used toilet paper and rolled yards."

I said, "And we went cupping and coning last week. To go cupping I drove up to Chic-fil-A and ordered and paid for a large lemon-aid then when the girl at the drive thru handed the cup to me, I grabbed it in center very hard and pushed a fingernail into the foam and made the drink gush out on the parking lot by crushing the cup. Emma and her friends posted the video on Vine of the server's reaction.

Then we said "Sorry" and drove off. Then I drove the teenage girls across the street to McDonald's and ordered a large ice cream cone and when the guy at the window handed the cone to me I grabbed it by the top of the cone and got ice cream all over my hand. The guy busted out laughing and the girls posted that on Vine. One of Emma's friends said I was cool and that her mom would never do that." Jill said, "It gets easier next year when Emma can drive. Hang in there. You are a good mom."

Some of my fondest memories with Jill were when our mom, Suzanne, would pick us up at the country club late in the afternoon. Then she would sneak the cook, Pearl, into the back seat of the Cadillac and drive her home. Mom always had a soft heart for Pearl and her having to walk a mile to the bus stop after working in the kitchen all day. Jill and I loved it because we knew that Mom would always put something in the trunk for Pearl to take to her grandchildren. It was usually items we no longer used, but it was very touching to see her give them to Pearl. Nothing was ever said, she just popped the trunk and Pearl took out the bag.

Now, thinking back just a few years and remembering the anguish and despair I felt every day, I have to thank God for my Mom. Her steadying influence and godly guidance helped me navigate feelings I never thought I would experience.

My mother instilled in me the grace to maintain my composure in the midst of difficulty. Visions of her elegance and demeanor would flash through my mind at the most challenging times, reminding me of who I was and where I came from. Her posture and cool-under-fire gaze could still the most rowdy child or bring silence to a room filled with conflict. I remember one Sunday in church Mom was sitting between Jill and I and we were startled when loud Baroque trumpets began to play. We immediately started giggling. Mom did not flinch one bit; she simply, nonchalantly, dug her fingernails into our thighs, with meaning, to silence her girls.

When Dad died, Mom had to handle all of the funeral arrangements as well as sell the law firm. More than once, I saw her stand firm, eye-to-eye with powerful men who wanted something she was unwilling to give. She held her ground and was quite a strong business woman.

I have watched her negotiate with men who thought she was less business savvy than they were, and saw them fall by the wayside as she gained the upper hand. After she was married, Mom learned the importance of being involved in the business decisions. That way, she was included and knew how the business was supposed to operate.

Both my dad and my mom accepted the responsibility for the decisions made about the business, and they both could defend those decisions if necessary.

Mom also accompanied him to his office so that all of the women in the office knew he was happily married. Mom would have thrown her high heel at any woman who thought about messing with her husband.

She was also a force to be reckoned with at home. When Jill and I were four and six, Mom had been asking our dad to be home more for dinner. It was very important to her that he spend time with his girls each night instead of working. He played golf every Saturday because she wanted him to have an escape from the office.

Once, when Daddy missed dinner for a week, Mom got Jill and me out of bed and in our pajamas, put us in the back of the Cadillac and drove to his office. He was still there so Mom got out of the car and threw a brick she had brought from her garden through the large plate glass front of the office. Then she drove us home and put us back to bed. We never discussed it, but Daddy began to have dinner with us more often. Mom always wore heels and was proper, but she was tough. Her nails, hair and make-up were always done up in a Southern belle meets Junior League kind of way.

When dad had his stroke, Mom remained by his side. Tenderly she cared for him like always since they were high school sweethearts. She told me that when she and Daddy first started dating, she knew he was the one she would marry. Daddy's legacy is far more than a successful law practice and two daughters. His legacy is also a wife who treated him with respect, both at home and in public. Truly, theirs was a special devotion and love.

What I saw modeled by my parents I wanted in my own life. Their love and commitment, their friendship and companionship, their trust and loyalty to one another was special and very rare.

I believed it could happen again and wanted it in my own life. Little did I know that, as steady as my parent's marriage could be, mine would become so dark and filled with despair that I questioned whether I was mentally going to survive

T.T. Johnson

I grew up in a home that practiced what it preached. My parents taught me to tell the truth by being truthful themselves. They showed me how to respect other people by respecting each other. They showered me with love, which enabled me to love others. They stayed together during good times and bad times, and through sickness. I understand genuine, heartfelt love and devotion because I experienced it.

So how could I become entangled in such a web of deceit, violence, rage and dysfunction? How could I, a properly trained southern belle, become the object of scorn and ridicule by one of the wealthiest and most influential families in Asheville?

The memories of the tragic, despair-filled days and nights caused such deep pain and suffering that it took years to be excised from my wounded soul.

Chapter 2

Like most people, my past is filled with things I can't remember and things I simply don't want to remember. And though I may not be where I thought I would be, I am where I'm meant to be—my past is neither my present or my future.

Despite the chaos and dysfunction that was present in my previous marriage, I held tightly to the belief that things would somehow improve. Though I had no idea how it could get better, a part of me deep down inside knew that I would come through. Looking back, certain events seemed to harden my resolve to overcome the darkness and emerge into the light of day.

I remember the shock I felt one day while working at a new job I had landed as a bank loan officer. My estranged husband, Ken, sent me a very terse text message that said, "Get a ride home, I took your Audi." Panic threatened to overwhelm me as I left my desk and hurried to the elevator. Running into the parking garage, I discovered that my Audi SUV was gone. Ken had taken the extra set of keys and driven my vehicle away! I had evidently left the extra keys behind when I moved out of the house. Travis helped me move the smaller items to my new rental house in my SUV and as he was handing out the light items for me to carry inside he grabbed a shower rod and said, "I have a big rod."

"Stop bragging and hand me something." I said. We needed the comic relief during this sad time.

My emotions were getting the best of me. I felt like the floor had fallen out from underneath me and I was sinking into a dark abyss. Walking back inside, my first stop was the ladies' room. I had to regain my composure before returning to work. Standing there looking in the mirror, I wondered how much more I could take. How many other nasty surprises lay in wait for me as the divorce proceedings went on? Ken was supposed to give me that SUV per the judge. Still reeling from the shock of what had happened, I called Belinda to come pick me up after work and drive me home.

Back at my desk, the contents of my SUV came to mind: my cell phone charger, yoga bag, the garage door opener and my favorite Chanel sunglasses. Ken was such a douche! My dad's original Monte Blanc pen and my work parking pass was in the cup holder between the seats. Why am I worried about stuff when Ken stole my SUV…he just stole it and drove away. I was feeling so angry. How low could Ken actually go? Did he sit around and think of new ways to be hateful to me?

I texted Ken immediately and demanded my SUV back, but he texted that he had already sold it. I told him that I wanted my belongings from it. He said that I could get them back in exchange for the engagement ring he gave me. The ring had his family diamonds in it and so it belonged to his family Ken texted me back. The ring was my property according to the lawyers and belonged to me.

Tired and broken, I agreed to give the ring back. After what Ken had put me through, I wanted nothing to do with anything that reminded me of him. Material things did not matter to me anymore, only relationships with people whom I loved were of value. Ken was a master manipulator and could lie without blinking his eyes. I was still reeling at how cold and nasty he had become.

I was shocked and surprised at the vindictiveness of Ken's revengeful behavior. My life was quickly unraveling as I faced cruelty and betrayal from the man I had slept beside every night for more than a decade. It was a bitter reality and a dreadful experience. Anxiety was draping over me again.

Nevertheless, I had to keep moving forward—Emma depended on me. So I cashed-in my 401 K and bought a used car that was several year old.

Going to work became a much-needed outlet for me. I was doing a good job and my self-esteem was beginning to return. One thing that bothered me, though, was the anxiety that I felt when families came in with their children. The small kids would often begin to whine or cry if their parent's business took too long. When that happened, I would feel a cloak of dread come over me and fear would begin to envelope me. I was tired of always being scared, and could not understand where this anxiety and fear were coming from. Ken was being difficult so I blamed it on him and the divorce.

During this time, I kept thinking about how worn out I was and how I hoped the anxiety would go away once the divorce was final. I was struggling just to breathe, it seemed, and I wanted to feel safe again. Through it all, I learned to minimize problems and not complain. I didn't want my family and friends to worry about me, but to myself I thought about how weary I was of always having to be on high alert and of being so afraid. I felt as if I could never lower my guard. My weight was dropping and I was getting thinner. It seemed I was just too nervous to eat.

My mother was unable to help me financially with the divorce, not that I would have asked her. After daddy died, she did the best she could to make a life on a limited income and live comfortably in Charleston with her sisters. She needed their emotional support. I was glad she could not see me this second.

I became very good at telling other people that everything was fine and I was doing OK. No one knew how fragmented I was and how much deception, betrayal and fear had seeped in my life. It still gives me chills to think about it.

As a mother and wife, I understand that sometimes women can tend to lose their sense of self. I am amazed at how little time women with small children take for themselves. Understanding this, I have been able to build a life for my daughter, Emma, and have gained control of my situation. We are very close and have a special bond, to the point where we can talk about anything, including sex. We have talked about boys many times, because it seemed as if she was always being pursued. I remember telling her once that sperm can jump, fly and live on a hard surface for five days. How is that for honesty? I remember Emma saying, "Eww, Momma, you are funny! I love you."

There was a time when people looked at me with such pity that I felt like I should comfort them. Nothing feels quite the same as someone with pity in their eyes saying, "Hello. How are you doing?" The conversation is strained from the beginning. I hated when people felt sorry for me.

Our lives are a web of blood ties, family secrets and parental influences whether we want it or not. Mine is no different. Cobwebs of lies had been uncovered and skeletons were falling out of the closets. My relationships were suffering as a result I simply avoided people for a while. My sister, Jill was my closest friend and I would not have made it without the grace of God and Jill looking out for me.

This life is not a dress rehearsal and most people get no second chance to redo their life, but I did. When Logan, my adopted son, came into my life, he forever changed me, for good and for bad. However, I have arrived at this place in life and I guess this is where I am supposed to be. Despite the challenges, I landed on my feet. And even after being lost during the dark years I recaptured a lasting love and belong to a happy, smiling family. Unconditional love is so important and I feel lucky to have it now.

"KATE! Aunt Jill is here to pick me up. I'll text you when we're on the way home."

I said, "Emma, I am your mother. Do not address me by my first name."

"Ok, Kate." Emma said. The she chucked up some deuces at me.

"I hate it when you put up a sideways peace sign." I said knowing that would irritate her.

"You are seriously ancient, bye, love you." Emma said.

"Love you more."

Emma was an easy target as a teenager and I enjoyed joking with her. We were at Walgreen's last week and she looks at the cover of the Time Magazine in the checkout line and said, "That's Morgan Freeman. How did he get rid of his freckles?"

"That is Nelson Mandela, goofball, Good thing you are pretty."

Memories seem to flood over me at times. I don't mind the good ones, but the bad ones can really bring me down if I let them. The worst part is second-guessing decisions I made then based on what I know now. I know it's irrational, but sometimes my mind just goes there.

My first husband, Ken, seemed to be everything a girl could want. He was handsome, polite, successful and educated. What I did not know was that he was also a master of disguise and very deceitful. So how can I now judge myself for decisions I made before I knew the truth?

Over the past years, I have discovered that many of my so-called "friends" were that way only when my life was going good. As soon as things began to go wrong, they turned and ran the opposite direction as fast as they could, never to be heard from again.

I also discovered that "truth" is relative in the minds and hearts of some people. The one person I thought I could trust the most, was also the most untrustworthy and least truthful! How does that work?

I discovered that money can hide all kinds of filthiness and that appearances are more important than wholeness. I found that family reputations are more important than integrity and character, and that duplicity is an acceptable tool to use in maintaining it.

Though I am on the other side of the gulf, I am still sickened by some of the things I saw and heard. Much of what I experienced in that marriage was completely opposite of the dreams I had going in. Though not as fresh in my mind, they have marked me nonetheless. I grew up in ways I never thought I would, doing things I never thought I could or should.

Some of those days are completely gone from my mind…either that or I have buried them so deep they may never surface. I like to think they are gone, never to return to haunt me. But in the midst of the trauma, warm, sunny, beautiful days still stand out.

One of those days was when I first laid eyes on my lovely little Emma. She looked like a little angel with perfect skin, so soft and tender and her little hands and feet. I never knew that a baby could be so beautiful. That day is burned into my memory and it never faded, even when I was surrounded by darkness.

Another day was when I walked into my first new house for the very first time. We had it built in a beautiful gated community with mature trees and spectacular mountain views. Our architect seemed to know exactly what I wanted and was able to deliver with a floor plan that was perfect. Our decorator seemed to know everything about me as she chose fabrics, paint colors and furnishings that perfectly reflected my taste and established my sense of home.

Suddenly my cellphone rang and jolted me back to the present.

"Hey, Jax."

"My leg is swelling and beginning to hurt so I am coming home and putting it up."

"Sure. The doctor told you to take it easy for a few days."

"I'll be home in a few. Love you." Jax said.

"Love you more. Bye."

Jax was playing golf and hit a ball into the woods and went to find it. While he was searching in the brush he disturbed a brown recluse spider nest. He quickly got out of the woods after finding his ball. Jax came home and later found his leg red with two black spots with clouds of white surrounding them. The red mark was right above his sock line on the back of his leg.

"I called Dr. Keith and am heading to his office right away." Jax said.

Jax returned home with the news the doctor wanted him to go to the hospital.

I told Dr. Keith no to give me oral antibiotics and that I would come to his office back in two days.

"Jax, why would you do that? You crazy fool!" I was upset and Jax could see it on my face.

"Nugget, I will be fine just relax don't get all riled up."

I got on google and looked up brown recluse spider bite. The pictures of the venomous spider bite were atrocious and it reads... *usually needs medical procedure to remove blackened, dead tissue.*

It says reactions vary. Some people have a delayed reaction and others an immediate reaction, and others no reaction at all... *for those with sensitivity to the venom the bite-site can develop into a volcano lesion...the damaged tissue becomes gangrenous and leaves an open wound that can be as large as a human hand.*

The Shattered Faberge Egg

"It's a very big deal Jax you need to take this seriously." I yelled.

"Dr. Keith took a culture of the bite and I will go back in two days."

That night while we were sleeping Jax spiked a fever and I woke up to him having chills and nausea. I said, "We are leaving for the hospital now." Jax refused to go. He said, "We can go in the morning. I need to take a shower and pack my creature comforts like my camera, computer, and phone charger so I can work from the hospital if they keep me."

Anger engulfed my body and I have learned this was the way to keep fear out. This was the way I dealt with fear. I got angry as a coping mechanism.

I had a hard time feeling my emotions and I was like an emotional iceberg. I did not know how to express any other emotion but anger because I was closed off emotionally and was like an emotional iceberg.

When I began to feel vulnerable, my past would haunt me because of the scars left behind I would insulated myself by blocking out my feelings.

I pretended everything was fine for so long that relearning to feel my feelings was tough. I loathed myself for allowing him to attack me and for pretending like everything was fine in order to keep up appearances. I hated living with someone with unpredictable behavior and the years where I felt so out of control.

It was very difficult for me to decipher what I felt and to stop using anger as my mask.

When I became anxious images popped into my head and I felt the urge to hide so to manage my emotional experiences I clenched my jaw and my muscles became tense. Because of the traumatic past I experienced I did not shut down like others when uncomfortable, I just got angry and pushed thru whatever crisis I faced.

I watched over Jax as he slept and waited for him to wake up. Jax was his own man and had been to 38 countries taking photographs. He was not afraid of a spider bite. The next morning red tracks were running up his leg and an infection had set in. Jill and I had already been on the phone discussing it and I thanked God for Jill's nursing degree. She was adamant he go to the hospital immediately for IV antibiotics and to have the wound surgically cleaned out.

"Jax, get ready it is time to go to the hospital. Do you want to be buried or cremated when you die?"

"Don't rush me Kate. I am not going to die. I am fine."

"I am FINE too, Freaked out, Insecure, Neurotic and Emotional, I continued,

I may kill you before the spider bite has a chance. Look at your leg. The red tracks prove it is infected and by the looks of it your balls will drop off if you don't get to the hospital."

Finally after Jax packed up half his belongings, we get in my car. He is the ultimate Boy Scout always prepared. I drove toward the hospital and my car slightly jerks forward and I looked at the gas gauge and we have run out of gas as a I steer to the side of the road. I put my head in my hands because I know Jax is going to say, "That's why I always fill up at a quarter of a tank."

I saw a police car behind us and jumped out and waved my arms like a crazy women. He pulled behind us and I run up to his window, "We are on our way to the hospital and ran out of gas and would you please take me to the 7-11 to buy a gas can and gas." I held up my Michael Kors purse and say, "I have money with me."

The officer agreed with a nod of the head. I opened the front door of the squad car and he says, "Ma'am, you will need to get in the back." I close the front door and open the back door and slide in the seat. I am startled that it is hard plastic seat with a cage protecting the officer. I have never run out of gas before and am embarrassed. We arrived at 7-11 and I try to open the door to get out. I attempt to open the door several times.

"Ma'am you can't get out of the back of the car. You, have never been in a cop car before have you?" He laughed at me as I said, "No."

He walked around to open the door for me and let me out. I was back with the full gas can in a flash.

We drive back to Jax who is still sitting inside my car. Once again I try to open the door of the squad car.

"Sorry." Shaking his head he walked around and let me out.

"Thank you officer, I appreciate your help."

We get to the hospital and Jill had already set up a direct admit from Dr. Keith's office and Jax was put on IV antibiotics immediately. The surgeon who drained the abscess and cleaned out the necrotic tissue from his leg said that Jax would be able to go home in a few days since the cultures came back clean.

Next to Emma, Jax is the best and brightest thing to come into my life after that dark, stressful time. When he showed up, I could feel the tension drain away.

Things are so different now. I feel safe, loved, valued and very special. In fact, it is becoming more difficult to remember the sad, bad times because so much good happens now. My life is not a wreck and I no longer feel abandoned. I am strong and not weak, bold and not timid, brave and not terrified. It is a completely different life than what I had before!

Nevertheless, I cannot completely separate myself from the years I had with my first husband Ken, not all of which were bad by the way. Good or bad, positive or negative, each day of that time with him shaped me into the person I am today. I read one time that a person is the sum total of all of their experiences. I believe that because I can see it in my life. Many things had to happen to overcome the odds thrown at me.

Because of the way I was raised, I entered college and then marriage with a particular framework with which to view the world. That framework was fine so long as I stayed within my element. But when I walked out of the door of my parent's home and went out on my own, my framework was tested and the weak points were exploited. I didn't think of myself as naïve, but I wasn't streetwise either. I was just me.

T.T. Johnson

Chapter 3

My sister, Jill, and I were raised in a tightly knit neighborhood where all of the families knew each other. All of the kids attended the same private prep school and every family belonged to the Country Club of Asheville. It was not as exclusive as the Biltmore Country Club in Asheville but it was our second home. On Sundays, the entire neighborhood went to the club after church to relax and eat a large buffet lunch. It was as if we were one big extended family.

During the summers, our mothers dropped us off at the club under the watchful care of the black kitchen and dining room staff. We participated in all of the activities at the club—golf and tennis camps and the swim team—and our dads played golf every Saturday. The 19th Hole was a men-only bar situated in the center of the club. Dot was our favorite waitress. Our parents loved her because she was strict and we minded her. She took up for every child and loved us all the same. Every day, she would wrap her arms around us and give us a big ole booby hug. We would sit inside and drink sweet tea, but were not allowed to be boisterous in the dining room. At the snack bar by the pool, we could "act a fool" because we were outside.

Our high school homecoming dance was THE event every fall. It was always a big deal, but I especially remember the first year I was able to go. Jax Harper had asked me to accompany him as his date. I had been in love with him since our first encounter at school, he just didn't know it. Jax was the cutest boy in school, until all the other boys grew taller than him in the tenth grade. He was about 5' 11" which was perfect for me since I was 5' 3". He said I was no bigger than a nugget and that nickname stuck.

Mr. Harper drove us to dinner and to the homecoming dance that night as he did not yet have a license. First they came to get me and then we planned to go to the country club for dinner before the dance. I was wearing a long red dress and a pair of Mom's high heel pumps. At fifteen, I had never walked in pumps and was a little unsteady. When Jax arrived at my home, I stood waiting at the top of the stairs to make my grand entrance. Both he and Mom were at the foot of the stairs and our black lab was curled up asleep on the landing. Carefully I started down the stairs but stumbled when the heel of my pump caught in the hem of my long dress. I lost my balance and rolled in a tumble to the bottom of the stairs, landing on the dog. He yelped and ran away while I jumped up with a red face. Not wanting to appear frazzled, I looked Jax right in the eyes and said, "I've been practicing that all day." He bent over and put his hands on his knees laughing hard. Both of the heels on Mom's pumps had broken off so she took me to her closet and found another pair. This was not exactly the way I wanted to start dating the boy who made my heart skip a beat.

I remember the first day of school that Jax transferred in from Texas. We were in the lunch line and I was wearing my cheerleading uniform and the guy behind me in line was taking his plastic brown lunch tray and using it to lift up my short cheerleading skirt and was exposing my tights which barely covered my behind. Jax watched him do it and noticed that I had no idea it was happening. It made Jax angry and steamed up. He came over grabbed the tray away then picked up the guy by his letterman jacket and lifted him up off the floor. Jax had been lifting hay bales all summer at the ranch. He said, "I don't think you want to do that again and if I see you try it you will have to deal with me." Jax told him, "You don't treat young ladies like that." The guy had a startled look on his face and left the lunch line. He said, "Harper, Jax Harper at your service ma'am." Jax had a megawatt smile the kind you could see under a blanket wearing sunglasses. I was feeling extremely self-conscious and experiencing the burning feel of infatuation for the newest student in school.

Jax made me laugh. He was so funny and he timed his lines perfectly. He was also handsome with dark hair and bright blue eyes, one of those guys who left you wanting more. I remember the first time he called me I was so thrilled my heart was pounding and I was anticipating him asking me out. Jax was a Texas boy from a ranch and he was always talking to me about something about deer or duck hunting. His family was very close; they only moved to North Carolina from Texas because of his father's job at the airline, which I later discovered was a cover story for their family secret.

Family came first to Jill and me as well, no matter what. This was hammered into our heads and modeled for us, and was an expectation Jill and I planned to live out for our parents. Our parents expected us to stay in the area after college and then get married and raise families here. We had a sense of belonging that came from this closeness that was very comforting.

One thing I especially liked about Jax was the importance he placed on his family. He was a hugger and a hand-holder, so our romance blossomed fast and our bond became very tight. He had a nickname for everyone, and me he called, "Nugget," because he said I was so precious.

Every moment of high school had a memory with Jax in it. Each morning he would come get me in his pick-up truck and have me slide over to sit by him. Then he would sing along with songs on the radio while he drove. He would hold my hand and use it as a microphone and then kiss the top of it. We had a little code that we used to say "I love you" when we were too far away to hear it. He would hold up three fingers which stood for "I love you." His index finger meant "I," the peace sign for "I love," and the Boy Scout salute (three fingers) for "I love you." He would rapid fire it at me thinking no one knew what it meant but me. This was a very special gesture that was too great to hold inside, so I told Jill and Joanne, swearing them to secrecy. Thank God they proved themselves trustworthy.

I loved being around Jax. He was always fun and he made me die out laughing like no one else could. It was the kind of laugh where you throw your head back and laugh with your mouth wide open. One thing that he did was stand behind me, wrap his arms around my waist and then kiss the back of my hair. He started this one night at a bonfire. I was cold so he became my human coat when I leaned into him and put my back against his chest. That was when he first kissed my hair. We wrote each other notes and put them in each other's locker at school we were always together and hanging out.

Jax was always there to listen to me and I loved him deeply. He would place his hand on the small of my back when we walked together, which gave me a sense of protection and comfort. He was my first love, the one I could never forget because the ties run so deep. There is just something about your first love.

We dated all through high school. After our senior year, Jax's father decided to move back to Texas to assist in running his grandfather's huge ranch. The family patriarch was ill with cancer and was unable to handle it with just Jax' uncle. That summer I went to visit Jax in Texas and had the best time of my life. He called me his dream girl, which sounded right every time he said it. Jax was all cowboy boots and country music, and riding horses came natural to him. He was a good marksman and knew how to handle a rifle. Seeing him on the ranch with his family revealed even more of the tie he had with his family. His dad worked for an airline, so while they lived in Asheville, he flew them to Texas every holiday so the entire family could be together.

I wondered if something was going on because the family had strict rules about going upstairs where all of the bedrooms were located. His Uncle Maxwell was never around after dinner and spent a lot of time in the master bedroom upstairs. It was not a topic to be discussed and seemed strange to me.

Jax had spent countless hours on the ranch over the years as he grew up. It was almost like he never really left. I was the only thing holding him to North Carolina, and I loved him too much to make him leave the place where he wanted to be so badly. When I boarded the plane home I knew that we would break up despite the fact that he loved me and I loved him. The love in his eyes for me was real, and he was the love of my life, but the distance was too great.

After a few weeks of being home I told Jax that I wanted to break it off. I told him that he needed to be in Texas with his family because they needed him there. I reminded him of how close they were to him and that his life was with them, just like my life was in Asheville with my family.

The Shattered Faberge Egg

That sad day was burned into my memory, and I can still remember how we both cried on the phone. It was over, my first big heartache. My mother taught me that the Southern way is to put my family first and not myself, so I let Jax go. He said that he would move back to North Carolina, but I told him "No." I would not separate our families. We promised each other to stay in touch and then began to laugh at our crying. I really expected to find another relationship and find another man who was like Jax.

Jax studied photo journalism at Texas A&M during the week, and then went home to the ranch on the weekends to work and help out his family. I think he chose that field because he knew how to tell a good story. As time went by he became very accomplished at photography. While in college we talked less and less and then eventually lost touch. Distance and busy lives had finally won. However, when we did talk by phone it was as if no time at all had passed. He still called me "Nugget." Nevertheless, our lives took separate roads, but I always wondered what he was doing and about his family.

Jax was definitely the one who got away, but then God says you are exactly where you are supposed to be. Why do things happen the way they do? Sometimes it is years before why is answered. Splitting up with Jax crushed my heart. We were both too young to understand how deep our connection was and that it was unique. He owned my heart, but I rejected him, only because I could not handle him telling me that the Lone Star State and his family were his one true love. We were loyal to our families and that was what we loved most about each other. Since Jax, I have compared every man I have met to him. No one has ever really measured up, but I was certain that I wanted a man who was loyal to his family.

My self-esteem centered around my sense of humor as I enjoyed making people laugh. I would always go for the big laugh, and Jax taught me how to tell a good joke. I was pretty, but was not stick thin like Jill. I was blessed with curves, but way before I wanted them. So I always felt curvier and used my sense of humor to cover up any insecurity that I may have had. This was something that saved me during the years I was covering up the chaos that happened behind closed doors. Being popular was also very important to me. I was never fat, just not as tall as Jill. Besides, I got the hair and I never let her forget it since she had legs.

I was often able to talk my way out of trouble. You know what I mean…flash a quick smile, a coy look, maybe a slight wink. One day as I was driving to school at UNC, I saw the flashing blue lights of a police car behind me. I pulled over and watched in the mirror as the officer approached my window. When he asked for my license and registration, I flashed my smile and pulled my shoulders back, thinking about how glad I was to have those curves. Then dripping with Southern charm, I pleaded with him to not write me a speeding ticket.

The officer told me to look inside the squad car and then said, "Do you see that man? He is my sergeant, and he will kick my butt if I don't give you a ticket." "Well," I said, "My daddy's going to kick my ass if you do." He laughed hard and wrote me a warning ticket.

Chapter 4

College was fun for me, and the University of North Carolina was so close that Jill and I could get home quickly. Jill started there the year before, so she kind of paved the way for me. We joined the same sorority and became ΣAE (Sigma Alpha Epsilon) little sisters. Ours was the first national fraternity to be established in the Deep South, having been founded in 1856 at the University of Alabama. The first semester I lived on campus in a dorm, and then Jill and I moved into an apartment. Throughout our college years, we earned good grades but still managed to have fun along the way.

One Halloween the ΣAE's had a frat costume party so we dressed up. Jill found an angel costume and we borrowed a devil costume that was covered in red sequins and came complete with a red pitch fork. I loved the red dress so I went as the devil and Jill went as the angel.

With all of the excitement of the upcoming party and rushing around to get ready, I didn't eat anything before we left. We met with another group at the Alpha Gam house and then we walked over to the party together. The girls giggled when they saw Jill and me dressed as an angel and a devil. We all wore costumes in hopes of winning the costume contest. I remember one of the best was a girl dressed as a brick house accompanied by a guy who was a "cereal killer." He had little cereal boxes taped all over his shirt. It cracked me up.

The band was playing too loud and it was very crowded at the party. When we arrived, we were each handed a red Solo cup full of "hunch punch." It was spiked with pure grain alcohol and mixed in a large garbage can that sat right next to a keg of beer. The reason it was called "hunch punch" is yet unknown to me, but it may have been because you hunched over when you threw up, and it left you with a nasty hang over. Anyway... the girls drank the punch while the guys drank beer and we all danced to the music.

That night we were introduced to a few people, and I saw Ken Burnett who I knew was from Ashville. The Burnett family was an old Asheville family that wielded tons of power. Their money came from the grandfather who was a timber magnate and land speculator. Everyone in Asheville knew of the Burnett's, but at UNC Ken seemed to rule the crowd. He had flunked-out of Clemson because he liked to party more than he liked going to class. He was a few years older than me and was back in school after taking some time off. Ken's family was very wealthy so he was there for a good time and was not particularly motivated to graduate. I think he was working towards a degree in spending money or whatever courses the financially privileged managed to pass.

The alcohol in the punch hit me fast and I got an instant buzz. It was past midnight and the party was in full swing when I poked my pitchfork at Ken and said "Do you want to go to hell with me?" Jill laughed and said, "Whoa! Satan called and wants his pitchfork back."

Jill could see that I was drunk, so she decided that I needed to go back to the apartment. She knew that the red dress, the crowd and the buzz were a disaster waiting to happen. Ken already knew everyone and was very friendly, so he offered to drive Jill and the "devil girl" home. Jill agreed, so he brought his car around, helped me get in, and off we went. Getting into Ken's car dramatically altered my life. It would be many years before I realized the full impact of that action.

When we arrived at our apartment, Ken helped Jill get me inside and then he ordered a pizza. He hung around and was very easy to talk too, so we drank coffee, ate pizza and laughed about everyone's costumes. Ken was dressed as the Mad Hatter from Alice in Wonderland and looked hysterical.

After that night, Ken and I started hanging out in a group with Mark and Maggie, and Jill and Travis. We had lots of fun going out to eat and to the movies; it was typical college behavior with plenty of free time and just wanting to have fun. Group dating was when the rich-kid was footing the bills.

The Shattered Faberge Egg

Ken had an expensive car, and he liked to drive me around and spend money on me. He also liked being a big man on campus. He was a perfect gentleman, almost to the point of being boring. He was tall and tan with big white teeth and had reddish brown hair. It seemed like everywhere we went Ken saw someone he knew. He was very social and always wanted to plan activities, but he was also very focused on his image and what other people thought of him.

Jill told me that Ken liked me, but I was not that interested. His family was very wealthy and he was so tall and attractive, the other girls thought I was crazy not to go for it. I thought he was kind of goofy at times, but knew that it was just his personality. He was so likeable, that we became friends first and grew closer over the school year. He was always making plans and I just went along.

As we grew closer, Ken opened up to me about his family and their expectations of him. He also told me about how his mother was always in the know and that he told her everything. When summer came we all moved back home with our parents. That was when I learned that Maureen Burnett, Ken's momma, was not happy about his new girlfriend...but I don't think she liked any girl Ken brought home.

Jill went with Ken and me as we drove up to the Burnett estate. When we walked in we found his mother, Maureen, and his father, Forrest, in the kitchen talking to his brother, Robert. According to Ken, his brother was the perfect son. Forrest favored Robert so Maureen was very protective of Ken.

The kitchen was large with cold granite everywhere. Likewise, I could feel Maureen's cold, icy stare as she scanned me up and down. She knew everything about me, but I knew very little about her. The introductions were formal and then Forrest and Robert left to play golf. Ken was not as much into sports as Robert; he was more into looking good and dressing well. He had the looks and Robert was the athlete.

Maureen was ice cold to me and very curt when speaking to me. I seriously wondered what I had done to offend her. Nevertheless, my southern upbringing kicked in and I made small talk. Finally, Ken took me to see the back of the house leaving Jill in the kitchen. Maureen Burnett cornered her and asked questions about our relationship. It was uncomfortable for Jill and she was angry when I walked back in from outside. Ken changed his clothes and we left to go out for the evening.

Later, when Jill and I got home she told me all about the conversation. "That woman is mean and cold. She really wonders if you are good enough for Ken." When I asked what Maureen had said, she told me that it was not *what* she said but *how* she said it that was so cold.

The summer was busy and Jill and I planned to work for daddy at the law office. Meanwhile, Ken's family went on their annual vacation to the beach. I am sure his mother was overjoyed because our relationship cooled.

That summer, Jax called and invited me to spend a few weeks at the ranch. I needed a job and wanted a break from the law firm. Jax said his uncle could put me to work ordering supplies for the ranch which paid more than I was used to making and I could bunk in the guest house. I eagerly accepted and booked my flight.

Immediately when I arrived, our relationship picked up exactly where it had left-off. I ended up staying longer than I intended, and our romance had rekindled. Being with Jax was all I ever wanted. It was the perfect summer of love and excitement.

Jax was fun to be around. He took me out to Duke's, a country music bar where we could line dance. It was great fun, so we went often and had a good time two-stepping. To make my ensemble complete, Jax knew that I needed some Wrangler jeans and a pair of cowboy boots, so he bought them for me. My new boots had some sparkle and a little red trim so they fit my style perfectly.

While I was there, one of Jax' great Aunts died. It was customary in his family for someone to always be at home to receive food brought to the family, so I volunteered to stay at the house while the family attended the wake. I got bored after a few hours and decided to look around inside the forbidden zone upstairs. When I went into the master suite, the first place I looked was the closet. On the top shelf were several white foam heads with wigs on them. I thought it was odd because I had never seen his aunt wear a wig. Then I saw size ten pumps and an assortment of dresses in size fourteen. Jax' aunt was very petite so I knew those could not be hers. Then it dawned on me. The woman I would see in the upstairs window after dinner was his uncle all dressed up. That had to be the big family secret. His uncle was a cross-dresser! I was shocked. Suddenly I heard the floor creak. I spun around to leave, but his uncle was standing in the doorway. Immediately my face turned red as He told me that no one was allowed in there. I just lowered my head and got out of that room as fast as I could while my heart was pounding.

The next time Jax and I were alone, I asked about his uncle's cross-dressing. He said that he found out while he and his brothers were in their room talking. In walked their uncle dressed from head to toe as a woman with a full wig, dress and make-up. He told them that this was how it was going to be from then on, and that dressing as a woman was how he relaxed and felt comfortable. Jax said that he and his brothers were shocked and very uncomfortable with the situation, so they stopped inviting their friends over to the house. He also said that the real reason they moved from Texas to North Carolina was because their dad could not accept his brother's cross-dressing. His dad moved the boys to Asheville to start a life away from their cross-dressing uncle. The only reason they moved back to Texas was because of his grandfather's cancer. Jax said that his uncle still "dresses" in private after dinner and that his aunt has learned to put up with it. It was a source of embarrassment for the family and Jax did not like to talk about it very much. His uncle was just that way and one of those skeletons you keep secret.

The next day my Mom called and I knew by the tone of her voice that something terrible had happened. She told me that daddy had suffered a massive stroke and that she wanted me to fly home immediately. Daddy's condition was very serious and time was of the essence. Jill had already booked my ticket, so Jax helped me pack and drove me to the airport right away. Because of the bustle at the airport, we didn't even get to say goodbye, but when I looked back Jax was flashing his fingers 1, 2, 3. His way of saying "I love you."

The flight home was a blur as I struggled with the emotions raging within me. Guilt was sweeping over me in waves, but I couldn't stop thinking about how I had wanted to get away from Daddy's office that summer. I wanted so badly to go to Texas to be with Jax. If only I had known this was going to happen... but how could I have known? Trying to rationalize my decision to see Jax just made things worse.

Jill met me at the airport and we rushed straight to Mission Hospital where Daddy was. I was very apprehensive about going in because I didn't know what to expect. Jill tried to get me ready by saying that Daddy was unresponsive, but nothing she or anyone else could have said would have prepared me.

I remember walking into the room in front of Jill, but when I saw the person lying on the bed, I thought it was the wrong one. I didn't recognize my own Daddy! He was lying still with tubes all over him. His face was drawn and pale and his eyes were closed. Dark black and blue circles were under his eyes and a breathing tube was in his mouth. Suddenly I felt very dizzy and had to grab the foot of the bed to keep from falling down. How could this be happening?

Mom looked exhausted. I could tell that every tear had been wrung from her eyes and there was nothing left. She jumped up to help me regain my balance and then took hold of me and began to sob from deep down inside. As her daughter, I had never before seen her so frightened and tired as in that moment. Jill immediately kicked in to big sister mode and began to help Mom and I get our emotions in check. Standing there in the middle of the room I wanted nothing more than to run away to some safe place, but there was nowhere to go.

Daddy stabilized, but never did regain consciousness. After ten-days in the hospital he was moved to a care facility where he could be monitored around the clock.

Though my last year of college was about to begin, I knew that Mom needed me at home. UNC Asheville had a new program in place where I could register for classes, watch them on TV and then mail my homework in. One day each week I had to go on campus for teacher consultation or quizzes, but I was able to study at home and finish my senior year while helping Mom out.

Meanwhile, Jax went back to Texas A & M to finish his photo journalism degree. All of the stress of my Dad's stroke, and me leaving so quickly, began to show in our relationship. Jax was very supportive of my decision to move back home, but time seemed to fly by. Needless to say, our relationship was on the back burner. Both of us were so busy with life we just seemed to drift apart.

Daddy passed away nearly three months to the day after having the stroke. Mom nearly fell to pieces. Looking back, I am so glad that I moved back in with her to help during this terrible, tragic time. For some reason, I was able to reconcile Daddy's condition much easier than Mom was. Maybe it was because I felt such a great responsibility to be there for her during this time. Through it all, Mom and I became extremely close and were able to talk with each other about anything that was on our minds.

One day I received a package from Jax. When I opened it, I found a note along with the cowboy boots that he had bought for me. My hands were trembling as I unfolded the paper to see what he had written.

Nugget,

Thank you for the wonderful summer. It was so much fun being with you. It was a very special time with my dream girl. I am so sorry about your dad and want you to be there for your momma and Jill. I feel glad we had that time together, but you need to stay in Asheville.
I love you.

Jax

Now it was my turn to cry great wrenching sobs from deep within. I knew that Jax was right, but that did not ease the pain in my heart. My love was so deep for this man that I could not explain it to anyone. I felt as if my life were tumbling out of control; first Daddy, and now this. How much more could I lose and still remain sane?

"Kate," Mom called, "Telephone."

T.T. Johnson

Chapter 5

"Hello" I said after taking the phone from Mom.

"Hi, Kate. This is Ken. What have you been up to?"

I couldn't believe it was him. It seemed like a lifetime since we had talked, and so many things had happened.

We talked for close to an hour, catching up on all of the news about our friends and family. Ken seemed sad when I told him about Daddy passing away. I didn't mention Jax…that wound was still very painful. But I was glad to hear Ken's voice. It was very comforting after everything else I had been through.

When Daddy passed, Jill and I helped each other get through the funeral. We each had a special relationship with him in our own way. As the oldest, Jill connected with Daddy in a very practical and almost business-like manner. She was always very logical-minded, which helped her relate to Daddy in his profession as a lawyer. My sister was my lifeboat always helping me stay afloat.

My Daddy was a big-hearted man who never wanted his girls to feel any pain and yet he trained us to be strong. When I about three, I found my red beta fish dead in its bowl so I ran crying to Daddy. He reassured me that the veterinarian could fix the fish so we took it to the clinic. After walking into the exam room the vet left with my dead fish and returned with it swimming happily in the bowl. I clapped my hands in delight. Later, as an adult, I learned that Daddy had called ahead and told the vet's office to run next door to the pet store and buy a replacement fish. The vet played golf with Daddy and they were close friends. This story always touched my heart and taught me to protect the ones you love. Daddy always said you need something to do, someone to love and something to look forward too. His wisdom and his devoted love helped keep me steady in the midst of storms that may have otherwise brought me down.

We loved to tell stories about Daddy, like how when he was late he would do funny things. One time he put his briefcase and a banana on the roof of his Mercedes and drove off. That morning when Jill and I left for school, we found the briefcase in the driveway and banana in the street. Another time he put his coffee in the car door cup holder then slammed the door shut splattering coffee all over his shirt and tie. Jill and I were eating breakfast when he came back in to change clothes. Mom just shook her head knowing how much he needed her.

The best Daddy story happened one morning when he thought he was home alone. After his shower, he walked nude toward the kitchen to get some coffee. Georgia, our housekeeper, was standing at the glass door about to come in. When Daddy saw her, he started running and slid on the wood floor hitting his forehead on the doorway into the dining room. He fell to his knees with blood dripping from his head and his rear end up in the air. Georgia witnessed it all and ran after him screaming, "Mr. Stenson! Are you ok?" Jill still laughs when we tell about Georgia seeing Daddy's business.

After Daddy passed, Mom had a real tough time, so Jill and I did all we could to help her work through her feelings of grief, anger and despair. We were both surprised at how angry Mom seemed until she told us one day how unfair Daddy's death was. He was full of life and very healthy and robust. In her mind, the stroke that took him was like an unfair sucker-punch, criminal in its fury and conniving in its timing.

One thing that helped shift Mom's attention was Jill getting married to Travis. True to Jill's dream, hers was a very southern wedding under a blooming magnolia tree. She was a beautiful bride and wanted a large traditional wedding, which gave Mom something to work on. Of course our parents wanted this for Jill as well, and had been preparing for it over the years. The saddest part of this wonderfully happy time was Daddy's absence. He always joked that he wouldn't give his little girls away to just anyone. He joked with Travis one time and threw a shot gun shell at him and said that if Travis ever made Jill cry the next shell would be coming at Travis a lot faster. We knew he really meant

The Shattered Faberge Egg

it. No one was hurting his girls. Privately Jill and I both cried because Daddy would not be at our weddings.

Watching Jill get married started me to dream more about getting married myself. My heart still ached for Jax, but that was over, so I decided to join a singles networking group and began to attend the monthly socials to see if I could find someone new and interesting to date.

The next week, my friend, Maggie, and I went to a social and joined a large group of twenty-something singles milling around and talking to one another. I enjoyed going because I could secretly watch others and pick up tips about what not to do! I also began to identify whom I would consider dating. Later in the evening I was taken completely by surprise when I came out of the ladies room and ran into Ken in the hallway. Ken gave me a big hug. As usual, he was smartly dressed and full of charm. As we talked, I learned that he was working for his dad in the timber business and was completely bored.

While we were sitting at a table talking, some strange guy came up behind me and put his hands on my shoulders. He was obviously full of himself because he continually interrupted us as we talked. Finally I could stand no more and told him to take his hands off of me. "Don't touch me." I said. The strange guy started making comments about how unfriendly I was and that I should be more considerate. I was infuriated and let him know that of all of the men there, he was the last one I would even look at, and if I did it was just so I could stay far away from him!

Ken laughed so hard I thought he was going to pass out. He was there with his friend, Mark, and asked if Maggie and I would be willing to bail out of the social and go to a movie instead. We were all ready to leave, so the four of us went to see a movie and then to a bar for a drink and to listen to music.

That night with Ken re-opened the door to our dating and we began to see more of each other. Ken called me every day and came over to see me. He promised me that his parents would not interfere like they had before, and that he was his own man. Nevertheless, his mother, Maureen, was terrified that I would trap him by getting pregnant, so she put the fear of God in him that I was only after his money and nothing else. While it was true that I enjoyed dating a rich guy, that was not the only thing that kept me with Ken. So, as our friendship grew, our relationship deepened in ways that we had not expected.

Ken and I went on lots of double-dates with Mark and Maggie, which added to the fun. The four of us went to dinner, movies, concerts and the beach as often as we could get away. We were all working and enjoyed going out to relax and have fun. I was not making much money and just moved into an apartment so having Ken pay for my meals helped me out a lot.

True to himself, Ken always made plans for the next big thing. He was very outgoing and liked being around a lot of people, so he naturally became the "event planner" for our excursions. He planned every weekend and was pretty much in charge of what we did. Ken was very good at remembering names and would drop a name here and there at our gatherings both to impress others and to gain favors.

The four of us loved spending time in downtown during Belle Cher, Asheville's Mardi Gras celebration. During that festival, we truly let our hair down and danced in the streets until the police made us leave. The party atmosphere during Belle Cher is unlike anything else in the mountains. Because Asheville is such a melting pot city, you can see street people mingling with the country club crowd, the straight-laced and the unlaced all in the same place dancing to their own beat.

We had to be careful, though, and pay attention to what was going on around us. Mark tended to get really wasted from time to time. One evening during the heat of the festival, he stepped aside for a shot of Jagger and was nearly rolled by two guys who wanted to fight. Mark got away, but they were so persistent we had to leave to keep from getting into an altercation. The last thing we wanted was a policeman taking Mark in.

That winter over Christmas our family decided to go snow skiing to reconnect after daddy died, so we all flew to Lake Tahoe and stayed at a ski-in/ski-out lodge. It was snowing when we arrived and fresh powder was everywhere. We were told that it was the best snow Lake

The Shattered Faberge Egg

Tahoe had seen in three years. On the first day, Jill and Travis went down the slopes first and then the rest of us followed. It was a perfect day of skiing.

On the second day, Mom and my Aunts stayed in the lodge by the fire drinking hot schnapps and telling family stories. Together they laughed and cried and then laughed some more as the day wore on. By five o'clock they were more than a little tipsy, so we hustled them off to bed for a couple of hours before dinner. Mom told me later that she needed that time with her sisters to finally let go of all of the stress and tension of Daddy's passing.

On day three it was colder and the wind was crisp. A lot of snow boarders were out and we could see them flying over the moguls and hills as we rode up the ski lift.

When we reached the top, Travis took off down the mountain with Jill close behind. I didn't see her go by, so I stopped and turned back to see where she was. Then everything went black. The next thing I remember is lying on the snow with people around me yelling and a warm sensation when I moved my head.

Someone had called the Ski Patrol and said they were on the way. When I asked what happened, Jill said a snow boarder jumped off an embankment and hit me in the head with his board. The injury was severe enough that I was transported by ambulance to the hospital. Jill went with me and seemed extremely worried all the way to the emergency room. My head was pounding, my hair was soaked with blood and my neck was numb. To prevent any further injury, the doctor put a halo on my head to stabilize it. All I could think about was how stupid I must have looked. Even though I had been hit in the head by a snowboard, I hoped my red lipstick was still in place.

I was placed in a medically induced coma for a few days and woke up looking at Ken sitting in a chair in my hospital room. When I saw him, I asked why he was there. He said that he rushed to be by my side as soon as Maggie told him about the accident. He had brought me flowers and a card to brighten the room and my spirits.

Ken stayed with me for the entire two weeks I was in the hospital and kept me company while my head and neck healed. The impact had cracked a cervical vertebra, so the doctors were being very careful to prevent further injury. After staying a week, my family went back to Asheville with Ken's assurance that he would stay with me. Mom needed to get back and both Travis and Jill needed to go back to work.

Ken made sure the hospital knew that his family was wealthy. For him, prestige and status were the keys to life and the pursuit of happiness. And, as my suitor and protector, he liked the way the nurses and doctors treated him as a result.

During that time in the hospital, with Ken being so thoughtful and diligent about my care, I began to appreciate his grand gestures and gifts. He always seemed to know how to put on a good show. Without realizing it, I was falling in love and enjoyed the attention Ken lavished on me. He had dropped everything to be with me, which spoke volumes to me about how he must have felt about me and our relationship.

The nurses came to know Ken after the first day when he began bringing them donuts in the morning. That must have helped, because I certainly received the best of care from them. When it was time for me to go home, Ken flew with me from Lake Tahoe, but insisted on upgrading our tickets to first class.

Upon returning home after the accident, Ken and I spent most of our free time with each other and did everything we could together. He enjoyed lavishing me with expensive gifts, which made many of my friends envious, but I was loving it! My family liked him and they told me that he would be a suitable husband for me. Ken was my closest friend, which was a big deal to my mother who only wanted the best for me.

The longer this went on it became clear that Ken would propose, but when? A girl can only hope…

Chapter 6

Every summer, Ken and his entire family vacationed for a week at Myrtle Beach. They always stayed at the Marina Inn at Grande Dunes, which provided the luxurious accommodations that Maureen insisted upon for the Burnett family. This was my first year to be invited and I was delighted to see that I had a room to myself. Maureen made sure that Ken and I stayed in our own rooms since we were not married. Ken's brother, Robert, and his wife had a private room as did all of the cousins, aunts and uncles that came along for the trip.

Aunt Evie (Evelyn Burnett, Ken's aunt) went on the trip every year and was very vocal about what happened, especially the dinner reservations and outings that she organized. Ken's father, Forrest, said she was "large and in charge." As the Burnett family matriarch, Aunt Evie carried the torch of who the family was and where they came from. She loved telling the story of how her husband died in a logging truck accident, saying "He died for the family business that he loved so much." You could almost hear Maureen roll her eyes and sigh any time Aunt Evie spoke.

Forrest treated Aunt Evie with respect and held her in high esteem. She came from a long line of old southern Democrats, and was a brilliant business woman. Evie was immaculate in how she looked, and she carried herself with dignity befitting the distinguished woman that she was. Aunt Evie always wore designer clothing with matching shoes and hand bag, all of which came from Niemen Marcus. Her ride of choice was a chauffeured Rolls Royce. She was the kind of woman who, when she looked down her nose at you over her reading glasses, would quickly put you in your place. Evie's sarcastic wit was funny as long as you were not the target, and it was usually spot-on. She said the things most people just thought. To say she was a powerful force in the family, and in Asheville and beyond, would be an understatement.

Try as Maureen might, Aunt Evie never liked her, even though she would try to impress her by putting on a good show in front of her. As far as Aunt Evie was concerned, Maureen just married the money, a point Aunt Evie always managed to make when the opportunity presented itself. She was all about the blood, and Maureen was not "of the blood."

With Ken always trying to one up his brother and Aunt Evie in competition with Maureen for Forrest's praise and attention, this vacation was exhausting. I felt like I was under investigation by the CIA with all the personal questions the family asked me, and wondered if I needed a security clearance to be in the inner circle. Nevertheless, I was quite competitive and determined that I would not be shut out.

My family was not poor and they raised me properly, but in Maureen's eyes I still was not good enough for Ken. She seemed even more standoffish to me on this trip, though she should have been accustomed to me after all the time I had spent with the family. I didn't like her attitude toward me, so I tried to steer clear of her to prevent an altercation. It was very uncomfortable, because I was still new enough to the family that I felt I had to "prove" myself.

Late one afternoon, Ken wanted to walk on the beach. It was right before sunset and we were already dressed for dinner. As we walked down to the shore, Ken took my hand and I noticed that his were very cold. I thought it was strange because it was so warm outside, but didn't think any more about it. After walking a short while we came upon a giant sand castle. Ken smiled as we got closer, and then I noticed that something black was hanging over the doorway. At first it looked like a bird, but as we got closer I saw that it was a scarf with something glistening on it. Then I saw an engagement ring tied to the scarf! My heart began to pound and I could barely catch my breath as Ken got down on one knee and took my hand. Then he lifted his head and with a look in his eyes like I had never seen before asked, "Kate. Will you marry me?"

My mind was reeling. In that moment I felt as if the entire world had come to a halt awaiting my answer. Not wanting to appear unstylishly eager, I quietly answered, "Yes." Ken rose to his feet and took me into his arms and embraced me. Then he placed the ring on my finger. Breathless, and with my imagination running wild, I looked at my new precious jewels. It was a two carat princess cut diamond with two round diamonds on each side.

Later I learned that the scarf Ken had used was the same one that Forrest used when he proposed to Maureen. Forrest pulled the scarf through the ring and then placed it in a long box. When Maureen opened it and saw the ring, he proposed. That was also when I discovered that the Burnett family placed great importance on a couple's engagement story.

Ken's parents had hired a security guard to watch over the ring and make sure nothing happened to it while we walked up. As soon as Ken proposed, the guard came over and congratulated us and then left. Ken had planned the proposal and all of the Burnett family, dressed in matching clothes, watched us from a dock overlooking the beach. Then the entire family came down to the castle to have pictures taken by a professional photographer hired to capture the event. After the photographer was done, Ken and I went back to his parent's suite and began to call friends and family to share the good news.

Everyone but me knew what was happening. I was completely surprised and wonderfully happy to get keys to the castle. What I did not know was that there were monsters in the moat and skeletons rattling in the closet!

Maureen was the first to tell me that the diamonds on the sides of my engagement ring were from her earrings and that the ring was now an heirloom that needed to stay in the family to be passed down. I was astonished that she was already talking babies and passing things down while I am still telling my family that Ken and I just got engaged!

Finally I pulled away to watch the sparkle of sunlight dancing over the water and to allow the serenity of the Grande Dunes to calm me. Too quickly though, the sun began to set and it was time to go to dinner with the crowd. The conversations that night were all about the wedding, the date and the venue. Aunt Evie, of course, said it would be held at the country club. Maureen piped in that it would be held wherever my mother wanted it, knowing that Evie would flip out if she lost any control over the event. Maureen sure liked to push her buttons. Little did I know that this was just the beginning of the wedding drama. Once again I felt like an outsider.

Planning the wedding turned into a feeding frenzy—it was almost like a college hazing, all of the women vying for their say so—everyone had their opinion and Ken certainly had his, too. But it was Aunt Evie who carried all of the authority in the family. She was "hell on heels" and refused to take "No" for an answer.

Wedding invitations were the first conflict we had. Aunt Evie and Ken demanded that they be engraved and not printed. I honestly didn't care, so I had two sets made, one engraved and the other printed. The engraved set, which was twice as expensive, went to all the Burnett family and friends. My family and friends received the printed ones. Maureen wanted all the replies sent to her house so she could track every RSVP. With all the Burnett control freaks involved I began to wonder whose wedding it was.

Forrest wanted to put their family name on the invitation right under my family's name. This was a very strange request as they were not helping to pay for the wedding. I refused to acquiesce to his request, which made him very unhappy. I wondered why he would want his name on his son's wedding invitation at all, it just seemed weird. Forrest was also unhappy with the newspaper announcement about the wedding as his name was printed with his first and middle names switched.

One day Jill called and we went to lunch. Over our salads, Jill asked me if was sure this was what I wanted. I quickly said "Yes," maybe because I was afraid to ask the question myself. Then Jill told me that she had never let me know what Maureen had said to her the first day we all met. When I asked why, her countenance became very sober as she told me that Maureen said I was not good enough for Ken. I was shaken. I knew that Maureen didn't really care too much for me, but I never suspected that she thought I was not good enough. Jill said she wanted to tell her that maybe Ken was not good enough for me.

Ken was such a showman it was hard not to like him. He knew that thin line between showing off and kissing up. Kate and I joked that he could win an Oscar. Then Jill said, "I wonder what Jax will say when he hears you are getting married." I quickly said that he was always traveling to a different country taking photos so he probably didn't know.

My sweet Momma did not need all of the Burnett wedding stress so I shielded her from it and let them take control of the planning. It seemed as if everyone in that family had an opinion and wanted to enforce it. Mom was spending more time in Charleston with her sisters and less time in Ashville which helped as well.

Flowers were another issue. I wanted white roses, but was concerned that they would be too expensive so I added in gardenias thinking that would lower the price of the bridal bouquet. Boy was I wrong. The price doubled! When the florist called Maureen, she went ballistic and asked what I put in the arrangement, so I called and changed it back to all roses. This made Maureen even angrier at me, so she changed it back. I just wanted to keep the peace so I went along with her decision. Besides, Jill wanted the story book wedding not me. I would have been happy with great pictures, a quick ceremony and straight to the honeymoon!

Ken had six groomsmen and I had six bridesmaids; they were a fun group. I chose red bridesmaid dresses from New York. They were stunning and looked good on everyone. Ken found an antique Rolls Royce to take us to the reception after the ceremony. He also made booklets for each member of the wedding party with times, directions and details of where to be. It was well-done, but who has time for all this planning? Jill and mom were helpful when we had the bridesmaid luncheon at our house. My cousins made everything and we thoroughly enjoyed the day. The conversation was light and bubbly as we dined on chicken salad and petit fours.

Just before the wedding I received a card and immediately recognized the handwriting on the envelope. There was no return address, but I knew it was from Jax. For a moment I didn't know what to do. I was hesitant to open it because of the feelings I might find seeping back in. I put it down on my bureau and decided I would wait to see what it said. Then my curiosity took over and with my heart racing, I opened the envelope and took out the card. It was a pretty standard card with a picture of a meadow of red poppies on the outside. On the inside Jax had written:

Dear Kate,

Sometimes, the only sense you can make out of life is a sense of humor. All I have ever wanted was for you to be happy. Congratulations. I love you so much Nugget!

Always,

Jax

    A range of emotions from longing to sadness to anger flooded over me. How dare he send this now? Jax was not even in Texas, he was off chasing his career as a photo journalist all over the globe. The last update I had was when he was in Nepal where he took a photo of two boys who were slaves carrying stone blocks in the Himalayas. The photo was published in Time magazine, which is the only reason I knew where he had been! He was well on his way to a very successful career in photography, always traveling and shooting the next story.

    The rehearsal dinner hosted by the Burnett's was way over the top, almost outshining the wedding. It included steak and lobster and silver domes…my entire family was very impressed. The whole event helped to refocus my energies on Ken and our wedding; it was unfolding very fast and was a blur of activity. Meanwhile, Ken was in his limelight and loved being the center of attention. He drank it in like fame, which made me laugh. He was truly having a big time with the whole thing.

    The next day, the Burnett's took my family out to dinner so Ken could announce our honeymoon destination. He and I had not discussed it, so it was a big surprise. Just before we ate, he presented me with a big box and told me to open it. I did and pulled out a bottle of water, a container of sand and a wind breaker. Then he made me guess where we were going. After a few missed guesses, he handed me a brochure of Monte Carlo and a photo of the Hermitage Hotel where we would stay. He was so excited that he laughed with anticipation and said, "We are flying into Nice and taking a helicopter to Monte Carlo." This was a place that I had dreamed of, so I smiled and told Ken how thrilled I was. He went on to say, "Our suite overlooks the water and has a view of the castle and all of the yachts docked at the port." I could imagine the beautiful blue ocean and the lovely setting, almost feeling the sea breeze blowing through my hair. My dreams were coming true!

While the topic of our honeymoon was still on the table, Ken reported that his brother, Robert, was a honeymoon baby, and was born shortly after Forrest and Maureen returned home. Forrest said that people at their church asked him when he and Maureen were married because she seemed to be showing just three months after marriage. That was how I learned why they said Robert was a honeymoon baby.

Aunt Evie had sipped a few glasses of red wine and was sitting next to me. Suddenly she elbowed me and said, "Bull. Maureen was already pregnant. We put their wedding together in three weeks. Honeymoon baby my ass!" Then she told me that was family secret #1 and that I might as well get used to it.

No wonder Aunt Evie was so hard on Maureen. Had she trapped Forrest or was it just an accident? Evie always accused Maureen by saying she didn't contribute to the family because she never worked a day in her life, meaning she never held a job. Maureen went straight from her parent's house to Forrest's house, and Evie never let her forget it.

What was I getting into? There was a big difference between dating this family and chaining myself to it by marrying Ken. Then Aunt Evie laughed and told me they had a "no return" policy once Ken and I were married.

Thankfully, the wedding went off without a hitch. The videographer was fantastic at catching everything on video. The stained glass in the church was offset by the dark mahogany benches. The candle light made the church look warm and inviting. Ken cried during the ceremony and I wished daddy was there.

I walked down the aisle on a path of red rose petals and it was perfect. On the back of the program was a letter that I wrote to daddy about how I loved Ken and hoped he was watching from Heaven and how I hoped we had his blessing. It was a touching letter and several people commented on how sweet it was to include it.

The reception was a great big party with plenty of food stations with all kinds of goodies. We cut the cake early and then settled in for lots of dancing. I could sense a thrill in the air and the hope for a lifelong marriage.

When it was time to leave, the Rolls pulled up outside the Country Club, and Ken and I started to hug everyone and say goodbye. Then all at once the confetti started flying. The groomsmen threw what seemed like tons of it in Ken's hair, so much that it went down his shirt and into his pants. It was hysterical! We both had glitter and confetti all over us. It was even in our luggage! After the reception, we checked in at the Grove Park Inn in Asheville to spend our first two nights as Mr. and Mrs. Kenneth Burnett. We slept most of the first day because the whirlwind of our wedding had exhausted us. Early the next day we went to the airport and on to our honeymoon in Monte Carlo.

Chapter 7

Finally we were on our way. Our flight out of Asheville was uneventful, but after we left Atlanta for London's Heathrow airport, we encountered some rough weather over the Atlantic, which left Ken feeling a little sick to his stomach. He was not nervous about flying but the turbulence bothered him and he just didn't feel good. . Right before we landed Ken puked in the pocket of the seat in front of him and then looked at me like nothing happened. Needless to say, I was glad when we touched down so I could regain my composure before leaving for France.

After leaving Heathrow, we flew directly into Nice. Upon landing, we climbed into a helicopter that Ken had booked, which took us to Monte Carlo and landed on the roof of the hotel! Tired, but very excited, we headed to our suite, where a welcome basket from Forrest and Maureen was waiting on the bed.

The staff had already been generously tipped, so they treated us like royalty and were at our beck and call. Just after we arrived, I called room service to order coffee and it was delivered very fast. I realized then that I could easily become accustomed to this type of service. This marked the beginning of my love affair with hotels and room service.

Ken had booked massages for us at the spa to help us relax after our trip. When we arrived at the desk to check in, we were informed that they had two messieurs available, a male and a female. We had asked for two female messieurs, but Ken told me to take the woman and he would be alright with the male. After our massages, we changed into luxurious robes provided by the hotel and went to lounge on the couches until we would be called back to the treatment rooms.

Later that day, we went for a drive in a rented Maserati. It was a beautiful day and the scenery was amazing. I wanted to remember everything, so I took pictures of the castle, the ocean and all of the magnificent yachts in the harbor. That night we ate dinner at Louis IV, and then went to the casino. Outside we saw some of the most expensive cars in the world so we parked right in the middle of them. Ken loved looking at all the cars, but security was very tight as the casino had some very high rollers inside. I remember thinking that this was the first time I ever felt poor.

When we returned to the hotel that night, Ken left me in the room to dropped the film off to be developed overnight for morning pick-up and then he went to do some shopping. I watched a movie and had room service. The next morning, after a delicious breakfast overlooking the ocean and watching the cruise ships arrive, Ken went to get our pictures. When he returned, he was livid because none of them turned out. They were overexposed because the camera had been damaged on the trip. I was shocked because I had never seen Ken so angry, and then surprised because he called his mother to complain and unload his frustrations.

That day, we went back to all of the original photo spots and snapped the pictures again using a brand new camera. I couldn't understand what the big deal was, but wanted to avoid Ken becoming angry again during our honeymoon. It was weird, because he actually made me change clothes while we were out so the pictures appeared to be taken on different days.

The last few days we were there, we enjoyed eating breakfast on the balcony overlooking the harbor and the Mediterranean Sea while Ken mapped out our activities. One day Ken chartered a yacht to sail us down the coastline of the French Riviera. Italy was visible in the distance and the beauty of the coast was outstanding.

Honeymoons have to end, and ours did too so we left for home. Upon returning to Asheville, Ken and I drove directly to our house. I had moved in weeks before the wedding in order to get settled. Ken's mother had arranged to have his belongings moved while we were away on our honeymoon. She said it was so we could walk into a functioning home right away, but it was actually a way to get a key.

She had been to the grocery store and left all the non-perishable items arranged on the counter so we could see exactly what she had bought.

The first thing Maureen said to me after we returned was that I needed to clean out my closets. My first thought was, "The only way you could possibly say that is if you looked inside every one of them." I decided to keep my mouth shut and went to the back of the house to be alone. Maureen and Ken continued to talk while I unpacked. I was scheduled to start my new job in a few days and wanted to get everything ready. Besides, I was eager to step into my new future as Ken's wife!

We had dinner with Ken's family that night. While we were eating, Aunt Evie started in again with the story about her husband dying for the business he loved. While she was talking, I looked over at Maureen and could see that she had checked out. I'm sure she was thinking "Here we go again." Forrest thought very highly of his sister because she was a brilliant business woman, so he would often let her retell the story. Her sarcastic wit was biting and no one wanted to be the target.

I wondered how Evie picked up the nickname "Tiger Shark" in the timber industry, so while she droned on with her story, I began to daydream about her as one. I had studied marine ecosystems in college and had learned about the tiger shark. I knew that it was a fierce predator, preying on anything in the water. I also knew that they are one of the most dangerous sharks for humans to encounter. I also knew that tiger shark embryos will often cannibalize their littermates in the womb with the largest embryo eating all but one of its siblings. I secretly called her "Aunt Evil," and thought, "Wow! That's 'Aunt Evil' for sure!"

Suddenly I noticed that conversation at the table had stopped and everyone was looking at me. Evie, with her piercing blue eyes and salacious tongue hoarsely said, "I see you've set aside this special time to humiliate yourself in public." Evie pushed, "Well, speak up Kate are you in a coma?"

I was completely embarrassed. My checks were burning and getting hotter. Did anyone else know how mortified I was? With a dry mouth I mumbled, "I apologize, Aunt Evie."

Forest decided it was time to bring me into the Burnett family business, so he took me under his wing to show me the ropes. He seemed to be very impressed with how quickly I learned the timber industry. One day he gathered the team in the boardroom and said: "Get a clear precise picture in your head of the exact place we want to be as a company." After the meeting he took me aside and began to explain the role he wanted me to fill. He explained that one of his primary roles was to find the right forestry consultant to select the best trees to cut. He wanted me to learn how to find buyers for the timber and get competing bids to obtain the best possible price. Ken had been tasked to do the job, but he was not a good salesman. He was gregarious and likable, but he had no follow-through to close the deal.

On the other hand, I was a natural at sales and had no problem asking for the order. When I had interested buyers I was able to successfully walk them through the sales process with little or no intervention from Forrest. I was also successful at getting sales by attending auctions where buyers would bid on the trees. At the end of the day, I would compare the different offers and name the winning bid. Then, after agreeing to the terms, I would have the buyer sign the contract.

Forrest liked my ability to sell so that the buyer never felt as if they had been "sold." I used consultative sale techniques, which meant that I approached a buyer as if they had a problem that needed to be solved. Then I solved their problem! This approach enabled me to knock out quotas in no time. Forrest bragged on my natural ability to sell to the whole family he had a new protégé. We became close.

Maureen and Aunt Evie however, were not pleased by my new-found success even though I made the company a lot of money. They were also unhappy that I had found favor in Forrest's eyes and did not like the protection that came with it. He had a new shining star, me, and he constantly talked about me.

This was a problem for Aunt Evie because she had always been the one who shined at getting things done in the company. At this point in her life, she wanted no competition or new talent that could knock her off her pedestal. Since the first sawmill was built in the United States, one hundred rules had been developed to account for the taper in all logs, the saw kerf (saw dust), and the procedure for removing wood on the outside of the logs for slabs. Evie was very knowledgeable of the rules and of the timber industry in general, and was in charge of keeping an accurate inventory of the trees.

Maureen was jealous of the attention Forrest gave to me. She had never held a job in her life and was truly a stay at home mom. Meanwhile, I was clueless of the alliance that had developed between Evie and Maureen against me simply because I did a good job at work. This alliance started in motion a series of troubling incidents for me at family gatherings. It was like the frog in the kettle story. You put the frog in while the water is cool and then place it on the stove. The frog doesn't realize the water is hot until it is boiling, and by then it's too late. Well, the frog was me!

The Burnett's celebrated birthdays once a month with a dinner and cake for the family members with birthdays. One Sunday afternoon the family had gathered to celebrate birthdays, so I called Maureen and asked her if I could bring anything. She told me "No" because we were going to have a pizza night.

When Ken and I walked into the house, we were greeted by Evie and Maureen, the "hot-flash tactical team." Right away, Maureen asked me to come into the kitchen to help her order the pizza, one large with everything including anchovies, and one large cheese. The one with anchovies sounded gross, so I repeated the order to Maureen, and specifically asked about it. She confirmed the order so I called the local pizza place and gave the order over the phone.

When the pizza arrived Maureen paid the driver and brought the boxes into the kitchen, calling everyone to come for dinner. Then she opened the boxes, picked up a piece of pizza and said, "Oh no. This isn't right, it has anchovies on it." Then she announced to everyone in the kitchen that I must have ordered wrong and told them to put anchovies on the pizza. Everyone moaned, and then Forrest said, "It smells like fish. I'm not eating that!" So Maureen "saved the day" by taking a honey baked ham out of the fridge along with some fresh rolls.

Then she said, "Take that pizza out to the trash and throw it away. It's stinking up the kitchen."

Immediately I questioned her and said, "You told me to put anchovies on it. I even asked you about it." To which she replied, "Then you obviously didn't listen very well, Dear." Instantly I knew that she had done this just to yank my chain. Then I thought, "So this is what it's going to be like." I could only guess what Aunt Evie thought, probably what an amateur I was.

Later that night, Ken and I had a long talk. When I tried to explain my side of what happened, he listened, but said nothing. He didn't even look surprised, like it was no big deal. I learned quickly that Ken told his mother everything, so she won again because he gave her a detailed version of how it affected me. I really mucked this one up. She made sure that we were alone when she told me to order the pizza. The old gal was smarter than I gave her credit for. My mind just doesn't work that way. I never go out of my way to plan revenge or humiliate people. I am fairly sure that Evie put Maureen through this type of hazing before, and now I'm tied to the whipping post!

A change of scenery was in order, so Jill and I decided to go get a mani-pedi and not let the Burnett family ruin the weekend. We went to the spa at the Grove Park Inn for the day and talked while we enjoyed a pedicure side by side. Since Jill was my guest, Ken had paid for her visit before we arrived.

Jill and Travis were pregnant with twins, a boy and a girl, so she was getting bigger every day. Mom was really happy and it was fun to see the nursery start to evolve with two of everything. Since they were expecting a boy and a girl they chose the names Sam and Shelby. I was comforted by the fact that Jill lived close to us and we could spend time together. She was a nurse and so was able to work when she needed or wanted to. It seemed like she always found the right nursing job to fit her needs.

Things continued to go well for me at work. I really enjoyed selling and loved the high that closing a deal gave me. I outshined Ken at work so much that I wound up helping him on the advertising side by hiring a marketing assistant who actually did Ken's job, but we never let anyone know.

All of Ken's clothes, except for jeans and t-shirts, were custom-made by the Tom Jones Company. The sales rep came by the office regularly and helped coordinate and maintain Ken's wardrobe. The rep would bring in the fabrics and make recommendations about what Ken should have made. At that time, we shared an office with two desks, so Ken would close the door so the young man could take his measurements. The whole process was really strange to me as I was happy to go into a clothing store and buy off the rack, but with Ken, it was nothing but the best. He was just that way, always bragging about something he had bought or ordered. He changed cars so often it was hard to remember what he was driving. He really liked looking at them and reading *Car and Driver*, which was his favorite magazine.

It was just like the Country Club. Membership is by private invitation only and then the candidate must be voted in before they can join. It was all very exclusive not inclusive. The Biltmore Forest Country Club was a Platinum Club of America and this award is only given to the top three percent of private clubs. The Burnett's knew the membership Director so we were very involved with membership elections. It was also a way for Aunt Evie to keep up with the gossip on everyone. She rubbed elbows with the elite and knew everyone, and everyone knew her.

Ken and I lived close to the club in a new neighborhood with lots of new construction. We were getting to meet new couples due to the pool parties and seeing others out walking their dogs. It was a planned community that was designed for a social environment. Every new owner had to be at or very near the same economic level or they could not get into the neighborhood. All the families were new and wanted to meet others. It was a community with a downtown that had restaurants and shops along a brick road with sidewalks. It was the perfect place to raise kids.

It was very important for Ken to impress other people, so he always made sure that when he met someone he dropped his father's name. It really started to bug me so I asked him once why he did it. He became angry and told me not to tell him what to do. I was surprised at his reaction and then wondered if he was really that immature.

Something wasn't right. It seemed as if Ken was becoming more critical of me. It was like a force field or an invisible wall between us that I could not identify or understand.

Chapter 8

During the first year of our marriage, Ken was busy checking things off the to-do list:
- ✓ Build our first house
- ✓ Join the Biltmore Forest Country Club
- ✓ Lease our first Mercedes
- ✓ Produce an heir

We both felt pressure from Ken's parents and Aunt Evie to "produce" an heir. In fact, "Aunt Evil" called me one day and asked, "When are you two going to have a baby?" Then she interjected "You surely aren't using birth control." It was really none of her business, but I told her that I had been off birth control for six months and nothing had happened yet.

Ken became very impatient the longer it took to get pregnant, so he insisted that I go to the lab for a blood test every month just to check. After 6 months we went to a fertility clinic, and our sex life became a science experiment consisting of a turkey baster and a brown paper bag of sperm. All of the drama caused me to think I was unable to get pregnant and it consumed my every thought. The fertility specialist said I had a very small uterus and that Ken had "slow swimmers." He said that getting me pregnant would be easy using artificial insemination, but carrying a baby was not a good idea. Nevertheless, we decided to move forward and have a baby.

When I received the confirming call from the lab that I was pregnant, I planned a surprise for Ken. I went to the baby boutique downtown and purchased pink and blue blocks and a baby swing. I spelled out "BABY" and hung the swing in a tree in the back yard. When Ken came home he saw the swing and immediately began to cry. He called his mother right away. She called Robert and he told Forrest before Ken even had a chance. There was no way to keep a secret in that family. At least I got to tell Mom and Jill first. Maureen was very excited and wanted to go shopping for a crib right away. Ken wanted a round dark wood crib so that was what she bought. It was a wonderful time having a baby shower and getting the nursery ready for the baby.

It was exciting to have a little girl growing inside my womb. My friends, Maggie and Belinda, were pregnant at the same time, so we were all "preggers" together!

Marriage was quite different from courtship. The entire experience of the engagement, wedding and honeymoon was so exciting and such a whirlwind of energy I wondered how we could keep that spark going. Ken's focus had shifted from our relationship to acquiring things and obtaining status. The infatuation stage of our relationship had ended and the early passion was gone. I was craving closeness, but that next level of passion that develops over time was not happening. For a while I blamed it on the fertility struggle we endured and how it took the passion out of our sex life, but now that I was pregnant Ken still would not touch me. Not even a hug. I felt like a walking incubator and that he didn't want to damage the cargo. We chose the name Emma for the baby and I was ready to be a mother but Ken's behavior was strange as he became more distant as I got bigger.

I simply thought this was a bumpy patch because I felt fat with my huge belly—it looked like I had swallowed a volley ball. It made me wonder: Can't someone make stylish maternity clothes? Mom had bought me a few things, but there is not enough hair and lipstick to cover the bump. Ken always had a crowd around him and was very concerned about what others thought. Therefore, he was naturally concerned about the clothes that I wore and how I looked.

The country club was a very important part of our social life. It was where we met friends for dinner, worked out and was a place where Ken could conduct business. In fact, we spent about as much time there as we did at home. Ken was very friendly and he had to know everyone. He was a name dropper and always knew the latest gossip. Because he was so affable, people talked to him and told him everything. That is how he knew the scoop on everyone at the club, everyone in church and even the people in our neighborhood. The Biltmore Country Club was founded in 1922 and was invitation only. Nothing like the relaxed country club Jill and I grew up in.

Ken treated me like a queen when we were around people outside of the family. He was so attentive that other women would become envious and want their husbands to be like him. However, his behavior would quickly change as soon as the car doors closed for the dreaded drive home. He would begin to nit-pick and criticize everything I had said and done. We were still new in our marriage and I didn't want to fight with him, so I kept quiet. Besides, I knew that I could never win an argument with him.

One night I wasn't feeling well and Ken really got under my skin. Maybe it was all the pregnancy hormones, but I unloaded on him: *"In case you haven't noticed the only person who doesn't think I am delightful and funny is you. Everyone likes me, and tolerates you. You are always showing off and dropping your dad's name into any conversation you can. Be your own man!"*

Ken was such a pampered pup that no one had ever served it back to him like I did that night. I was furious and just had to say what was on my mind. We drove in silence to the house and then I immediately got out and went to the master suite to take a long, hot bath. The bubbles almost spilled over the tub and the candles I lit put a beautiful glow all over the bathroom. I needed to feel pampered that night because there was something wrong. That evening at the club I ran into JoAnne Taylor. The first thing she asked was if I had heard that Jax was married. I felt like she punched me in the belly. Flushed with embarrassment and a host of other emotions, I hurried to the ladies' room and quickly found a stall and shut the door. Ken couldn't see me like this, especially because it involved Jax!

At home in my bubble-bath, I could begin to sort out my feelings. In my mind I knew this was silly. Of course Jax would get married. I wondered what she was like and how Jax was doing in Texas. Finally I began to relax in the warm water and wondered if his new wife knew what a catch she had. Deep inside, I knew that Ken was no Jax, but I had somehow thought that money would help fill the hole in my heart that Jax left behind. It was still a very tender place. I learned then that you never forget your first love.

Jax and I were both at fault. We loved each other too much to pull each other away from our families. I always thought that Jax would lose respect for me if I left my family to be with him. He was so loyal to them. In fact, he was loyal to a fault. Now we were married to different people and I was pregnant with Ken's child. I have a different life now and am happy to be with Jill and my mom. Asheville was the life I had chosen so it's time to get busy living.

The next morning Ken and I had our coffee in silence before getting ready for church. We attended a large church and Sunday mornings were always a big social event. Both of our families went there, so not showing up was out of the question. Slowly I drug myself out of bed feeling really strange, but I got dressed for church anyway. On the way to the "pep rally," what Jill and I called church, I felt my water break. I told Ken and he immediately freaked out. He was worried about the leather seats in the Mercedes instead of me! We actually laughed when I bit his head off while screaming "Get me to the hospital!"

When we reached the ER, he left the sedan running, jumped out and rushed inside in his usual "all about me" way. The attendants came and helped me in right away when a nurse noticed the blood. I woke up to Ken sitting in a chair by the hospital bed.

This was the second time this happened in my life, except this time there were no flowers and something was very wrong. When I asked about the baby, I noticed his parents in the doorway and Jill and Mom at the end of the bed. Ken said "Emma is in the ICU" then he said, "I have bad news." I glanced at Jill and then braced myself. Ken said, "We can't have any more children." Then, with his voice cracking and tears running down his face he said, "The obstetrician had to do a hysterectomy because your uterus was torn and you lost a lot of blood. It was life-saving surgery."

For a long time I just lay there looking at Ken with mom holding my hand. In some ways I felt numb and in others I felt angry and cheated. Overall, though, I was filled with joy that Emma was safe and doing well. Finally, after a long silence, I said what was foremost in my mind: "God has a plan."

Emma came out of the hospital perfectly healthy. She was a delightful baby and so full of life. Neither Ken nor I could have planned anything as special as her. To top it off, she was smart and was speaking in full sentences by 18 months. I poured every ounce of myself into our little daughter. I discovered with her that I was a good mother.

Emma had ringlets in her dark hair and flawless creamy white skin. She looked like a little Snow White. I loved styling Emma's hair. As it grew, I would gather it into a tiny ponytail and tie it with a big bow. Her big blue eyes framed her tiny face. I hired a painter to put Venetian Plaster in the dining room—it was all the rage at the time. The painter said in his English accent, "You are the spitting image of your mother." Emma looked at me and asked, "What does that mean Mommy?" "It means our faces look alike." I said. Then she said, "Except mine is smooth." The painter and I both smiled.

Ken wanted big birthday parties for Emma and Christmas was always over the top. He even hired a Santa Claus to come by the house each year to see Emma and take a photo.

Every year Ken had me take Emma to a professional studio and have pictures taken at a garden. Then we chose the perfect shot which the photographer stretched onto canvas and turned into a beautiful print. Though it was expensive and showy, we always had a current portrait of Emma over the fireplace. Ken loved it.

Every year our Christmas cards featured a picture of Emma created by the same studio. One year the owner of the studio called Ken and asked if they could hang a canvas photo portrait of Emma in the studio as an advertisement. Of course Ken was excited to do it. He told everyone about it and was so pleased to have been chosen.

Ken probably sold more sittings for that photographer than any advertising they could have purchased. He was the best at spreading the word. Emma's portrait hung in the photographer's shop window so we had to walk by and see it every time we went downtown.

That year, Ken threw Emma a huge birthday party with horse rides for the kids and a cupcake boxed for each child to take home. Two hundred people were invited and Ken had the photographer there taking pictures. He had a picture mailed of each child on the horse sent to the parents just to make it over the top. It was close to being ridiculous.

After Emma turned three-years-old, Ken began talking about a brother for her. He wanted another child, but specifically he wanted a son to carry on the family name. His parents were pushing for adoption and thought it would be a very admirable thing to do. He checked into a Christian adoption agency and told them we wanted a "Gerber" baby, healthy with no mental or physical issues. This involved additional money and screening, but Ken insisted.

Ken never asked what I wanted about anything. It was always what he wanted and I went along. Besides, I had Emma and didn't need anything else. She fulfilled the love that I needed in life. Once I heard in a sermon at church that "love does not divide, it multiplies" so I knew I could love another child; my heart had room. All of our friends were having baby number two so it seemed natural to be in this stage of life.

My mother called from Charleston and told me that adopting a boy would be a great idea so no little girl would have to be Emma's "ugly little sister." Emma was such an easy child I figured this mothering deal was easy. I was a good mother and followed all the advice that the baby books put out there.

Then the day came when Ken received a call about a blond haired, blue eyed, one-year-old boy who was being placed for adoption. If the birth mother signed the papers he could be ours in three weeks. We decided to name him "Logan Parker Burnett." Logan was already his first name and we didn't want to confuse him by changing it. Ken stayed in touch with the counselor at the adoption agency and we hoped for the best. We figured if it was meant to be then it would work out.

Ken and his mother followed every move that the adoption agency made. Later I learned that she saw Logan while he was still in foster care before we ever got to meet him. Ken knew but he kept it from me.

It didn't seem to matter too much. I was so involved with Emma and spending time with my friends and their children that Ken and Maureen didn't get on my nerves much anymore. I was very happy and content with my life choices. Emma had filled a void that Ken was either unable or unwilling to fill. He can only focus on himself and I had to accept it and realize he was unable to give me the support and attention I needed. Besides, he was a great father to Emma.

Emma and my family filled me with joy. I was more fulfilled than I could ever remember, and now we were preparing for Logan to join our family. Emma was very excited about her new baby brother and asked, "What will he be like?"

T.T. Johnson

Chapter 9

My life dramatically changed after Ken and I adopted Logan. With Emma and then Logan, it seemed as if I was always on the run to somewhere. Ken was gone much of the time so I leaned on family and friends for support. I thoroughly enjoyed being a mother to Logan and Emma, although I had little time for myself.

When Logan was two-years-old, the dreaded "terrible-two's" seemed to come in waves. However, in spite of all the tantrums and belligerent behavior, he still loved to snuggle and wanted me to carry him.

Logan carried his blanket everywhere—he called it his "blank-blank"—and came unglued if he did not have it. One morning at church, the nursery worker said he could no longer bring his blanket because he was using it as a net to capture the other children and then tackle them to the ground. The episode embarrassed Maureen, so she became emphatic about us weaning Logan off the blanket. He was a thumb-sucker and would hold his blanket in the other hand as a comfort item. It was huge so we began taking it away by cutting it into four big squares and continued to cut it up until it was in small strips. This solved the problem of the big blanket as Logan would carry strips with him.

One day I was talking with Jill on the phone, telling her about some of Logan's escapades. He had flushed a ball down the toilet and while the plumber was repairing it, Logan picked up the Lysol foam bathroom cleaner and sprayed it into his mouth. He also had knocked over the hamster cage, threw his shirt in the pool, and stuck his finger in poop while I was changing his diaper. He put a tic-tac up his nose, painted his hands red with fingernail polish and stained his teeth and lips black by biting an ink pen refill. It seemed that his behavior was becoming more extreme. Jill, my ever-patient sister, just listened. She had no idea how much I needed that from her.

That Christmas, Jill and Travis had a family picture taken with their 6-year-old twins, Sam and Shelby. Sam had a black eye because Logan had punched him. The first day of Mom's Day Out, I had dressed Logan in a Polo shirt and shorts, and then I went to brush Emma's hair. When I returned, I found him holding a black magic marker that he had used to mark all over his face and inside his ear. Emma and I roared with laughter. I just could not let Logan out of my sight for one minute.

Logan's erratic behavior continued to escalate to the point where I became very weary of people telling me it was the "terrible-twos." Compared to Logan, Emma was an angel and extremely easy to parent. He was wild and all boy. In fact, I had never seen a boy with more natural sports ability than him.

We bought a little basketball goal for Logan so he could learn to play. Looking back, I can see that I just needed to keep him active to use up some of his energy. I was worn out by not sleeping well at night and with all the messes that he made. He did random things like climbing on the sink and squirting lotion everywhere, or taking his juice box and squeezing it to watch the juice squirt all over the kitchen. I went to use the restroom once, and when I returned, he was outside standing on an overturned garbage can using scissors to cut the bushes. The backyard was fenced so he was very safe, but I had to watch him every second.

Emma was not at all like Logan. She was obedient and I could leave her unattended watching television for fifteen minutes or more at the same age. I knew boys were different, but I wondered if something else was going on, like ADHD.

As time went on, Logan became more uncontrollable and had daily tantrums. He had never been a good sleeper and had started to roam at night. One night the neighbor came home at two a.m. and found Logan outside in the driveway with his new flashlight riding his tricycle. When Jill asked me how Ken reacted to that, I told her that he was furious, at me! Jill didn't understand and asked why he thought it was my fault. "After all, he was at home sleeping just as you were" she said.

I told her that neither of us heard him go out the door, and that the garage door had been left open.

Ken was furious that a neighbor had seen this, so he turned the doorknob around on Logan's door and locked him in his room at night. Then he installed locks high on the doors and we started using the alarm system at night. Jill was shocked that all this was happening and asked why I hadn't said anything to her about it. I explained that Ken didn't want anyone to know. He wouldn't even talk with Logan about his behavior because he blamed me for not being a good mother. This led to more arguments because I believed I was doing everything possible to correct Logan's behavior. Jill was my confidant. I could always talk to her about anything, and it was comforting to have someone that I could trust on my side.

Mom was with her sisters in Charleston and Jill had become more of my voice of reason.

Logan would often wake up at two a.m. screaming and calling out. I always ran into his room so he wouldn't wake Emma, and then spend hours getting him settled back to sleep. I was exhausted. Our pediatrician, who was also our neighbor, would laugh at me and say he was just a typical two-year-old boy. There was no way I could explain everything in a five-minute routine doctor visit.

Going anywhere in the car became an ordeal. When I put Logan in his car seat he would scream and bite my hands. Emma was in school, so I shared a carpool with three other moms. One day, Logan spit on one of the little girls as she was getting in the back of the SUV. I was horrified. After the first week of carpooling, two of the mothers dropped out because of his behavior. The last day that we had a full car, Logan took off his tennis shoe and threw it at me hitting me in the back of my head. All of the kids laughed so he threw the other one. The next day, the windows of the SUV were open a bit and he threw his shoe out the window. I had to turn around and go get it. Emma thought this was hysterical, but not me! From then on I locked the windows and stopped putting his shoes on him until we arrived at our destination. Ken was of no help with the kids it all fell on me.

I couldn't help but think back to the day we adopted Logan and how excited we were to get him. Ken was very happy to have a son to carry on the family name. It was also very exciting for Emma to be getting a baby brother.

Logan was too much for his seventeen-year-old birthmother and she was unable to raise him alone. She was living with her grandparents and the grandfather was sick. With her grandparents unable to help any longer, they placed Logan up for adoption with a well-known national agency. The counselor handling the adoption rode with us to Louisiana so we could meet with the birthmother and her grandparents. Logan's birthmother looked very uncomfortable and had very little to say.

When I told Logan's mother what a gift it was to adopt her baby boy, she looked at me and said, "Thank you." Then I told told her that God had taken a hard situation in her life and turned it into a good situation in ours. Ken was trying not to get choked up so he talked very little.

Logan's biological family handed him over to the counselor and then left. I saw as she held him how tiny he was for his age. His white blond hair was fuzzy and had some static in it, but there was no sadness in his blue eyes and he seemed at ease with us. And, true to form, his blanket was close by and his thumb was in his mouth.

When the counselor handed Logan to me, he settled in and let me hold him. Logan did not yet speak and was a very cute child. Ken was crying and his parents, who covered cost of the adoption, were very excited that our family was now complete. Logan was a very loving child and we were amazed at how he instantly took to all of us, especially Emma. He loved chasing her around.

We themed Logan's room with sports paraphernalia including a golf club, a tennis racket and a boat oar hanging on the walls. The curtains featured metal grommets and were printed with basketballs, footballs and soccer balls with blue denim trim to match the bedding. Toys were everywhere—any little boy would have been in heaven.

At first, Logan called everyone, "Dada," no matter who they were. It was really cute. He woke up often during the night, so I would go in with a juice cup and rock him back to sleep. We knew the transition of changing families would be hard on him, so we didn't worry when he woke up crying.

The first few months were fantasy-like, filled with love and family hugs. Emma was fascinated with her new brother and was very helpful. She loved playing with him and watching Disney movies together. One night Logan kept hollering "Mommy! Mommy! Mommy!" I went in three times to check on him, kiss him goodnight and told him to stop yelling "Mommy." He kept on doing it for twenty minutes while I waited for him to get tired and stop. Finally I lost my patience and said, "Do not say Mommy again!" and then walked out of his room and shut the door. Suddenly Logan yelled out, "Kate! Kate! Kate!" I couldn't help but burst out laughing.

Logan was a smart little boy and we loved him so much. Nothing is the same as when your little boy's face lights up when he says, "Mommy" and then wraps his tiny arms around your neck. Logan had a loving, gentle side that could melt your heart. He was a very affectionate child who had the ability to be very giving and kind. That is until something switched and he got mad.

Emma was very kind to Logan, so we tried to help him understand that he needed to be kind to her as well. He was so hard to deal with that it took most of my time, leaving very little for Emma. Ken took Emma to birthday parties, church events and school functions while I stayed home with Logan. Logan was just too difficult to take anywhere. I had to watch him like a hawk because he hit others and spit at them. When he became angry he would try to bite me.

During this time, our marriage lacked the luster it used to have. The worst part about it was that Ken seemed indifferent to me, which was very difficult to endure. He was hard to please and expected me to care for and control Logan.

One weekend we went as a family to a pool party three houses down. Logan had a hotdog and a hamburger and wanted to walk with his plate, but I said, "No." Immediately, he grabbed the plate and threw it in the pool and then watched as buns floated across the pool beside his chips. A familiar hot, red burn came across my face as I grabbed him and marched home angrily. Meanwhile, Ken and Emma stayed at the party while I endured his tantrum all by myself.

By the time I carried Logan home, I was sweating. Needing to cool off, I decided to jump in the shower so I took him into the living room to watch TV. About the time I got a good lather going I saw Logan out of the corner of my eye as he entered the bathroom. Suddenly I felt anxious because he had a very mischievous look in his eyes. Then he ran to my closet that was next to the shower and began throwing my high heels over the shower door. In seconds he had thrown several pair in while I was screaming at him to stop. Then I began to cry. The water was off, I had shampoo in my hair and soap was burning my eyes. As I cried, Logan began to laugh, and the harder I cried, the harder he laughed.

Where was this going? What is happening in my beautiful little family?

Chapter 10

Logan was becoming more problematic with each passing day. His erratic behavior made it difficult to know when he was at or near a tipping point where he would become violent. With Emma, I could look into her eyes and get a feeling for where she was emotionally. Not so with Logan. He could turn instantly and become uncontrollable and then turn back again just as quick.

After one exhausting day, Logan and I had fallen asleep in the rocking chair. I was bone-tired so it did not take much for me to drift off. I couldn't rest though, because my mind would not slow down. It was becoming more apparent that something was wrong with Logan. I knew that something had to be done, but what? Then I began to feel guilty because I dreaded spending every day with him. I gently picked him up and laid him quietly in bed, praying that he would not wake-up.

Desperate for answers, I went to the computer in the kitchen and began to research ADHD in young children. After reading the symptoms, I decided to make an appointment for Logan with a child psychiatrist. I knew that Ken would not support taking Logan to a shrink, but I was determined to do it anyway. Besides, Ken was never around and did not have to deal with Logan's outrageous behavior. When I told Ken about the kicking and the biting, he just blamed me and said that I should be stricter. I tried to explain to him that spanking Logan did not work; it only made him madder and harder to calm down so I refused to do it. Besides, I never had to spank Emma as a stern voice was all it took to correct her behavior.

One Sunday morning a nursery worker at church stopped Ken and asked him not to bring Logan back to class. She told him that something was wrong with Logan because he would bite and hit the other children, which caused the parents to complain. He had already bitten a little girl on the cheek and the parents had demanded that Logan be removed from the class. The nursery worker explained that it required one full-time person just to watch him, which made it difficult to properly watch over the other children. As an alternative to the nursery class, the children's ministry director said the church would provide an empty room for Logan so long as one of us stayed with him.

During the church's Easter egg hunt, Logan ran around stomping on the eggs while the other children collected them in their baskets. When I asked him what was wrong he hissed, "I need to hit somebody." As we were leaving, a woman wanted to exit through the large glass door, but Logan would not let her open it. When she pushed on the door handle, the door opened and Logan fell down. Then he jumped up, ran over to the woman and spit on her dress. When Ken told him to say he was sorry, he pinched Ken and spit on his pants. Furious, Ken carried Logan straight to the car, put him in the car seat, and spit in his face. Then he yelled, "So, how do you like that?" When Emma started crying Ken tried to comfort her, but she was so upset it was no use.

All the way home, Ken yelled at me about Logan and what had happened. I tried to explain to him that with Logan I didn't even know what normal was. He was a small child, but I had to watch him every second of the day as if he were a toddler. I felt like I was always on high alert.

Ken was so infuriated that it turned into a three-day argument that I had no chance of winning. Fighting with Ken was like fighting with a dead dog. There was no way to win or breathe a breath of fresh air into it. Finally Emma said, "Daddy is a grumpy butt." Poor Emma, she was so easy-going and such a joy but she felt the tension in the house between Ken and me. It was hard on her with Logan requiring so much of my energy.

After the Easter episode, Ken allowed me to take Logan to see Dr. Minton. Once inside the psychiatrist's office Logan ran over, sat in the doctor's lap and gave him a giant hug. He squeezed his neck very hard, in fact, he squeezed too hard. When I gathered Logan from Dr. Minton's lap, he put his arms around my neck so tight that I actually walked back to the chair without having to support him in my arms.

The Shattered Faberge Egg

I showed Dr. Minton how Logan clung to me and explained how he wanted me to hold him but would then become very hyperactive. Dr. Minton stated that Logan had been overly affectionate with him and asked if that was a pattern. I told him that I never knew who Logan would hug, whether a UPS man or the mail carrier. I was worn out from living with him so I looked right at the doctor and said, "Medicate him or medicate me. I am toast." Dr. Minton asked me many questions and I spilled every detail that I could think of over the last year.

After about an hour Logan got bored and started walking around the office. When I got up to stop him Dr. Minton said to let him continue because he wanted to observe him. The doctor sat quietly watching while Logan played. A short time later, Logan was ready to leave. When I told him that we were not finished, he reached over and pinched me on the arm. I pulled away and said, "No sir! We do not hurt mommy!" That agitated Logan and he began to kick my legs. I took hold of him and tried to give him some juice from a sippy cup, but he took it and threw it at the wall causing a vase on the shelf to fall to the floor and break. The doctor said, "STOP, Logan!" and was able to divert him with a plastic robot.

Helplessly, I looked at Dr. Minton and asked what was wrong with Logan. He said, "It doesn't matter what you call it, no doctor will label him or diagnose him until he is in his teens." Then he said that the medication available for very young children would be the same no matter what diagnosis he made. After listing the pros and cons, Dr. Minton prescribed Risperdal to be taken twice a day. He said this would help calm Logan so that he could take a nap and go to bed at night and sleep. Dr. Minton explained that Risperdal had been effectively used in children to treat irritability and serious behavior problems. He also said that tantrums and aggression starting so young was a major concern so he wanted to see Ken and me with Logan in two weeks.

Logan left with a cherry sucker in his mouth and I called Ken to tell him what the doctor had said. Immediately Ken put a lid on anyone knowing that Logan needed medication. His family had a lot of pride so it was necessary to keep it secret. While I waited for Logan's prescription to be filled, I asked the pharmacist what the drug was used for in adults. He responded in a whisper that it was an antipsychotic drug used to treat bipolar and autism. At this point, I felt like someone had slapped me in the face. No one knew what was wrong with Logan, but I began to fear it was something worse than ADHD.

Dr. Minton asked me to keep a chart of Logan's behavior after we began the medication. The first night he slept through the night, but I still woke up because it was something I had done every night for a year. I had the listening ability of a trained assassin, waking up when I heard any noise and always wondering if it was Logan. The medication worked great for about two weeks, but by the time we were due to see the doctor, Logan was acting out.

One minute Logan was sweet to Emma and I was able to give him a bath and play with him. The next minute he was trying to bite and push her. When the meds wore off, he was extremely hyper and ran all over the house. Once, when I asked Logan to eat something, he threw the TV remote at my head and screamed," I don't like you." Then he spit at me and screamed until he was hoarse.

Emma's favorite time of the day was when Logan was asleep. She and I would lie on her bed and talk about her day. That was when she got one-hundred-percent of my attention and loved every minute of it. We would laugh and giggle and play a game called Velvet Hammer where we pretended to lightly hammer on each other's arm. If you let the hammer drop you got tickled. It was a time for Emma to be a little girl. I would hug her tight and thank her for all of her help. My sweet little school girl and had it tough with her adopted brother. Her friends stopped coming over to play because of Logan, so she always had to go to their homes to play. The other mothers really did not want their daughters around Logan since he was so difficult. It was a stinging source of embarrassment for me.

Ken was distant and offered very little support, finding excuses to be at work more often. My social life was over since I was chained to Logan. I felt alone and wondered if this was somehow my fault.

The next few months were filled with doctor appointments for Logan and driving Emma to and from school. To help out, my mother would babysit Logan and Emma when she was in town if Logan was already asleep when she arrived. It was the only break I got until we hired a nanny. I finally told Ken, "I would let Satan himself babysit Logan if I thought I could get a break for an hour. I can't take it anymore and I can't do this alone."

The nanny didn't stay very long, quitting after just one month with Logan. One afternoon Jill came over to watch him for a few hours while I ran some errands. When I returned home I started talking to Jill and told her that I was discouraged because Logan was so difficult to handle. How could I love someone so much and be so anxious of them at the same time? I never knew what Logan would do next. Jill agreed and said that being with Logan was frustrating she wanted me to take him back to the doctor.

Finally Ken and I met with Dr. Minton to go over the logs I had kept of Logan's behavior. Ken was loaded with questions and he wanted answers. Dr. Minton told us that Logan was "too young to make a diagnosis for anything. We just have to experiment with medications to see what works." Then he doubled the dose of Risperdal to four times a day and sent us on our way. Logan was not even in school yet and he was already on medication. I tried not to think about it anymore.

Forrest and Maureen wanted to take Logan out for ice cream one Saturday so they set it up with Ken. I took Emma to her soccer game and Ken stayed home with Logan waiting for his parents. He wanted to impress his father by acting as if he was involved with Logan, so he gave Logan his Risperdal early to insure that he would be calm. Unfortunately, he fell asleep in the booth at Baskin Robbins with his grandparents. Forrest had to carry Logan to the car and Logan slept all the way home.

Maureen was very upset and told Ken that there was nothing wrong with Logan except that we were over medicating him. She had Ken all riled up so I walked into a storm when I got home. He demanded that we take Logan off his medication to see what would happen, so I called Dr. Minton to ask his opinion. He said "Well, it might be good to see what happens." Little did I know that Dr. Minton knew exactly what would happen to Logan once the drugs left his system.

After twenty-four-hours without his medication, Logan had a screaming fit that lasted for almost an hour. He screamed "I hate you" at me until he was hoarse. Then he threw a full glass of orange juice in Emma's face, locked himself in the bathroom and kicked the door so hard it made dents in the wood. I called Ken, pleading with him to come home and help. When Ken arrived, he grabbed Logan by the shirt as he ran by, strapped him in the car seat and then drove through McDonalds so that Logan could eat something. The change of scenery seemed to help him settle down. Logan was exhausted so Ken drove around until he fell asleep. After that episode, Ken decided to put Logan back on his medication, and I had major increase in respect for Dr. Minton. That was the proof that Ken needed to see that the medication helped Logan's mood and leveled him out.

Deep in my heart I knew that something was terribly wrong. It made the back of my neck tight because I was so worried. Logan's sudden outbursts of energy and violent behavior troubled me. The problem was that I didn't know how to face the fear threatening to overwhelm me.

Chapter 11

In the midst of everything that was going on with Logan, Ken decided that he wanted a new house. His sights were set on something bigger that had an outdoor kitchen and a full entertainment area by the pool that had glass walls that slide open for parties. We already lived in an upscale neighborhood and Ken wanted to maintain that status, so we stayed in the neighborhood and had a custom home built with everything he wanted. It was nice to have a distraction from Logan's issues.

The area where we lived was in very high demand, so we were able to sell our current house in just two days. When it was time to move, Ken hired a company to pack and move everything so I was able to skip work and just watch the kids. Although the house was beautiful, I couldn't help but wonder if our lives were going to be spent obtaining material things. There was always someone with a larger house or a nicer car and it seemed as if Ken was always trying to "one-up" them. He always had the latest and greatest but was never content.

After we moved in to our new home, Ken decided that he wanted to have a big party to celebrate. There were some final touches that he wanted fixed before the party so the house was full of workers. During this time, I stayed home to make sure that everything on the punch list was done correctly. The last thing I wanted was Ken angry. He was very meticulous and extremely hard to please.

The wallpaper in the entry hall bath was not to Ken's liking so he hired a painter who specialized in faux-finishes to come in and change it. Logan was running through the house and getting in the way so I decided to take him to Chic-fil-A while the painter was there. As I was telling the man that we were leaving, Logan ran in and punched him right in the groin. The poor man doubled over in pain and made a horrible gasp. I apologized profusely and explained that we had adopted Logan and that he had some issues. The painter stood, looked me in the eye and said, "Well maybe his mother should have had an abortion." I left the house with tears running down my cheeks and my heart full of pain for this child whose problems seemed to be mounting. What a horrible thing to say!

The next few days at our house were rough. Logan had gone into the garage, climbed into Ken's sedan and colored all over the leather seats and console with an ink pen. I called the car Ken's "girlfriend" because he loved it so much. He was so angry when he found out what Logan had done that he spanked him with a belt, which left bruises on Logan's behind. I was upset that Ken had struck Logan out of anger. This child already had enough against him and did not need that type of punishment.

After that episode, Ken hired Vera, an ex-basketball player and coach, to be Logan's nanny. She was over six-feet-tall and had a very muscular build so she could handle Logan when he behaved badly. He did better when it was just him at home without many people around, so Vera home-schooled him when he was in a good mood.

One morning Emma came down ready for school and sat down to eat her oatmeal. She seemed very happy that morning, and looked cute in her school uniform. We were chatting away about her day when suddenly Logan ran into the room with an white extension cord in his hand and began whipping Emma on the back with it. I immediately yelled at him to stop, but then he began hitting me with it. The weight of the plug on the end made this a real weapon.

When I grabbed the cord and jerked it out of Logan's hand, he bit me on the arm leaving deep teeth marks above my wrist. It really hurt. Then he took off running and knocked over a lamp. When I went after him, he turned and spit on me so I yelled, "No! No sir." This only made him laugh and he began pounding on my legs and stomach with his fists, all the while growling and making monster noises. Then he ran and climbed up the outside of the staircase screaming, "I don't like you." A short time later, he jumped off the stairs and sat down to watch TV and seemed much calmer.

After Logan went upstairs, I went to comfort Emma. She was crying and traumatized by the whole situation. Thankfully, Vera arrived at that moment. She could tell that we had had a bad morning with Logan by the look on my face. "Awful early for an episode" she said. I just shook my head which told it all. Logan's "episodes" marked our days. We just tried to live in between them, never knowing when he would have another one.

It was time to leave for school, so I wiped Emma's tears, picked up her lunch box and my purse and we walked to the garage. On the way to school, I kept telling her how much I loved her and how sorry I was that she had been hurt. Emma didn't seem that upset anymore by Logan's behavior. His episodes were becoming more frequent and she was growing accustomed to them. She and I bore the brunt of Logan's behavior. Ken was gone all the time, leaving early in the morning and not returning until late at night, so he only experienced an occasional episode on the weekend. My tolerance for discomfort was high and I am beyond my comfort zone with Logan. I am not sure what to do at this point.

On Logan's birthday Ken invited his entire family over for a pool party. I cooked and we had a Batman-themed birthday cake. Logan, over-excited and very hyper, was running around dressed in his Batman suit making the cape fly behind him. He was having a great time and was fun to see him playing. Logan was pretending and he said Spiderman and Superman were flying with him. He had a vivid imagination.

When Evelyn, Forrest and Maureen walked in, Jill whispered in my ear, "Dominating, Spoiled and Neurotic have arrived." Robert was already there with his kids and Travis was with the twins, Sam and Shelby. Then I heard Aunt Evil call to Logan, "Come here sweetheart. I want to take your picture." Logan ran over and said, "I am not sweetheart, I am BATMAN!" then stopping only long enough to pose for one picture, he ran off.

The other kids were ready to get in the pool, so I had Logan change his clothes in the kitchen. He was behind the counter and kept saying, "Hurry! Hurry! Hurry!" because he wanted to be the first kid to jump in the pool. Maureen and Forrest were sitting at the counter and could see Logan changing into his suit. She noticed the bruises on Logan's behind, but didn't say anything at the time.

Soon all the kids were in the pool. Music was coming out of the faux rock speakers in the landscaping and the LED lights in the pool were changing colors. The kids were having a great time.

The adults were sitting at tables around the pool watching the kids swim and play. Out of the corner of my eye I noticed that Maureen and Evelyn had cornered Ken and were in deep conversation. Then they called Emma out of the pool and began examining her back. I moved closer and heard them ask Emma how she had gotten the bruises on her back. She told them that Logan had hit her with an extension cord. Maureen said to Ken, while looking at me: "It looks like my grandchildren have been abused." I told her that I refused to dignify that accusation with a response. Then Evelyn got in the middle of it and called Forest.

Evelyn demanded to know what had happened to Emma. About then Logan got out of the pool; his bathing suit was sagging revealing the bruises on his behind. Evelyn came unglued and began spewing fire and threatening Armageddon. Ken did not come to my defense at all; he just let her carry on. I exploded and said, "Ken spanked Logan, it was not me." Everyone was yelling at once and hammering me with questions. I was devastated that Ken would not speak up and tell his family how sick Logan was. I trusted him to defend me and tell them the truth about what was happening with Logan. Ken would not admit that he bruised him over the ink in his car and instead blamed me for spanking him. This ripped a hole in my heart and I felt betrayed.

This whole situation was crazy and I felt like I couldn't breathe. Jill came out and stood protectively by my side. Everything I knew about fairness went out the window as I realized how full of surprises Ken was when it came to looking good in front of his family. The Burnett's had no idea how hard dealing with Logan had become.

Jill took me inside and said, "You are on your own when it comes to dealing with Logan's problems."

We set the food out and I tried to hide the hurt in my eyes. It was an uncomfortable meal and everyone left right after we ate. As Jill and I were cleaning up she said, "Kate, you need to get wiser, and no more taking the blame." She explained to me that I needed to document Logan's outburst in a journal and on the camcorder for protection. I realized then life was ever changing and that I must adapt because it will never remain the same. It was a good thing Mom was in Charleston and had to miss the party.

I felt trapped, sealed in a vault. Sadly, the vault was my life. "God help me because I feel helpless. I have sacrificed everything to take care of Logan and protect Emma." Wondering if Emma would ever know the amount of effort it took to protect her was on my mind and that kept me going.

Jill's advice was right on, so I began videotaping Logan's rages and documenting his outbursts in writing. I took photos of bruises and bite marks so that I could take them with me to his doctor visits along with my journals.

Ken decided to have a behavior counselor come to the house to evaluate Logan. I was sure it was Aunt Evil's idea; he would never come up with that on his own. The counselor's name was Pam. After introductions she sat down at the kitchen table and asked Logan to come sit by her. She explained that she had some games she wanted to play with him. He was interested for about five minutes and then became bored. When he started to get up Pam said, "Logan we are not done, sit down please." Logan jumped up, slapped the glasses off her face and while running off said, "I hate you, you stupid idiot."

Pam got up and with Vera and I behind her, followed Logan back to the playroom where he was standing watching TV. He had picked up two matchbox cars and had one in each hand. Pam instructed Logan to come back to the table because she was not finished. He screamed "No!" and threw both cars at her. She was standing close enough that he hit her with both cars. I heard Vera mumble under her breath, "Direct hit."

Vera went to the other side of the room and I blocked the door to contain Logan in the room. He was very agitated by this time and kept yelling at us to go away. Then Vera said, "I've got this. You two go in the kitchen." Pam and I went back into the kitchen and Logan returned to his TV watching, still standing in front of it. Vera knew that Logan needed to be by himself so we left him alone.

Pam said she couldn't believe how difficult Logan was. No one had told her that he was so explosive. I gave her details on how Logan behaved and about his outbursts. Then Pam asked me how I was handling all this drama. I said, "Like a gem, sparkle on the outside, non-crushable on the inside" referring to a saying in my journal. Pam said that I was what they called a "treatment parent" and that I needed more help and a break from the situation. She said she would write up her report on what she saw and make some recommendations.

Suddenly I missed my mom and realized it was time to reach out to her for help.

Chapter 12

I was at the end of my rope. Logan had pushed me to the edge of my sanity and I was completely frazzled. Desperate for help, I called my mother in Charleston and immediately began crying when she answered. Between sobs I blurted out, "I just can't do this one more day!" Then I told her how bad everything had gotten with Logan and with Ken. Mom listened patiently and then told me that she would come over and stay for a week or two to help me and to be there for me.

Suzanne Stenson was a rational woman and very compassionate. More than ever I needed her sensible, warm personality. She had always been very stable, which I really needed more than anything else at that moment.

When mom arrived, there were hugs all around and then Ken took her bags upstairs to the guest room. Logan happened to be in a loving mood that day and wanted me to hold him, so I was carrying him and he was hugging my neck. I told mom how much I appreciated her doing this and how happy I was that she was there. She said she was happy to do it then went upstairs to take a bath and get settled in. Emma was very excited and looked forward to going to get a manicure with her Mimi.

I was downstairs with the kids when suddenly water came pouring out of the vent in the dining room. I screamed for Ken to come and thankfully, the water stopped after a short burst. Ken was instantly furious. He called the builder and told them that someone needed to check this out first thing in the morning. Ken was so meticulous about the construction of this house that he had hired another inspector to inspect everything the builder had done and then wanted everything fixed to perfection.

Ken had already ripped into the builder because the wood floor in his office had gotten wet when water came in through the French doors during a storm. They had to replace the flashings around the doors and Ken was furious about it. What a perfect way for my mother's visit to start.

The next morning the builder sent four men out to find out what happened and discovered that the plumbing in the guest room was not connected. When my mom unplugged the bathtub, the water ran into the wall through a vent then down into the dining room.

Ken sent a very harsh, nasty letter by email to the builder and signed both of our names. The builder was very apologetic and worked to have the tub repaired in two days. While the workers were there, Mom supervised them while Vera watched over Logan.

I was able to spend some much-needed time with Emma so we went for a pedicure, something we had been doing on special occasions since she was very little. It was our special thing to do together and we both loved it very much.

The next day mom took Emma out for ice cream after school. While they were out, Emma said, "Logan has HGTV." Mimi said, "Don't you mean ADHD?" Emma said, "Yes" and then went on to talk about a mean girl at school. She told mom that she didn't even let the girl's Barbie live in the same house as her Barbie when they played. Mom laughed thinking it was good for Emma to have a normal outing without the stress of Logan.

Mom saw that Jill was right about it being very hard for me to relax. Ken was always angry about something and Logan was a "hot mess." My life was in constant chaos. I never relaxed and rarely even sat down.

Emma, bringing mom back to their outing, said she wanted more sprinkles on her ice cream. Mimi smiled and said how pretty she thought Emma's eyes were. She asked Emma a few more questions and gave her the attention she craved. They went shopping for headbands and then drove back.

My mother quickly noticed that things between Ken and me were not what they seemed. He was of no help with the kids and did nothing around the house. It really ticked her off to see me holding down a job while trying to keep Logan in line and Ken off of my back. It was any mother's nightmare. She knew I was stuck in a war zone and knew of no way to help.

One night after the kids were in bed, mom was upstairs when she heard Ken berating me. Curious, she stopped at the top of the stairs and listened.

Ken was going off on me about the color of some of the grout. He accused me of changing it on purpose against his wishes. I tried to tell him that I had nothing to do with the grout choice, but by then he was mad and yelled, "I wanted the travertine to have a darker grout and you knew that. Never do that again! Don't ever change something I want." Ken was outraged and had become completely unreasonable. I kept telling him that I did not change the color; the men who laid the travertine had matched the grout.

Meanwhile, Suzanne was thinking, "I would tell him to jump in a lake." She knew that Ken never treated me like this when other people were around. She was beginning to see a side of Ken that she had never experienced. There she was with a front row seat to my life and she did not like what she saw.

The next morning when she walked downstairs Ken was already gone. She looked me right in the eye and said, "I heard Ken getting on you last night. Just let it be said that I would have told him to go jump in a lake."

I was humiliated. "Mom, it is just easier not to argue with him. I can't win an argument with him when he gets so mad about such little things. Besides, I don't have the energy to fight after dealing with Logan all day."

"Logan woke up screaming last night" Suzanne said.

"He has night terrors and wakes up like that often. He usually goes back to sleep or comes down and gets me. I hope it didn't keep you up long" I replied.

Then mom asked me when Logan's next doctor appointment was scheduled. I told her that it was in two weeks. Then she said that he seemed worse and asked, "Do you think he will grow out of this?"

"Sure he will" I said, while trying to stay positive and pretending that everything was fine. I had turned that into an art form because I knew deep within my soul that Logan would never get better. He was not alright and unable to go out to eat in a restaurant because he could not sit still.

"Mom, the last time we took him to eat out with the Burnett family Logan put three rocks in his pocket from the potted plants in the front of the restaurant. Once we were seated Logan took out the stones and threw them across the room. One of the stones hit an elderly woman in the forehead and her daughter came to our table and cursed me out. It was humiliating. Ken had me take Logan home in the car and had Forest and Maureen drive him and Emma home after they finished eating. Why did I have to leave with Logan? He has two parents."

"Kate, when Ken is demeaning to you in front of Emma he is teaching her what level of respect to accept from the man she will marry one day."

Then my mother began to probe deeper, and expressed an interest in how Ken treated me in the bedroom. I told her that Ken rarely touched me and showed no interest in satisfying me. She then suggested that I make an extra effort in this area to help the marriage.

That remark went too far. "I have, mother, and I have pleaded with Ken for us to see a counselor. He told me that I was just too fat to have sex with" I snapped.

"Kate. No! You have a tiny waist, and you are the only woman I know that can finish 'The Insanity Workout.' You ran a half marathon last year. That is a ridiculous excuse."

Mom was right. I laid my head on her shoulder and began to sob. She held me tight and rubbed my back just like she did when I was little. Then she said that the stress of raising Logan and the strain it had put on our family might be why things were so tough. Then she added, "I am so sorry baby girl." Mom could see the wear and tear of my life in my eyes. The blue sparkle was not as bright. My life was in chaos and the world was throwing sand in my eyes it was hard to focus on what I wanted.

The next day mom took Emma shopping for clothes after school, which made Emma very happy. When she came home, the first thing she modeled for me was the fancy new dress that Mimi bought for her to wear to the Candle light service at church on Christmas Eve. Mom suggested that we put the Christmas tree up early since she was there to help and thought it might cheer me up. I thought it was a fabulous idea. Emma loved this part of our family tradition, and it would be fun to do it all together.

Vera volunteered to get the plastic bins out of the attic, so I put in a workout tape for Logan and me while we waited. It was one activity he enjoyed doing with me.

We put a tree up in the playroom for Logan so that he could put super hero ornaments on it any way he wanted to. Then we put a formal tree in the living room by the fireplace, arranging it so the lights would be visible from the street. Christmas is the best holiday and putting up the trees helped put me in a much better mood. I love Christmas and enjoy wrapping gifts in matching paper to add to the festive look. This was my absolute favorite holiday and time of year. Red was my favorite color so it was the theme of all of my decorations.

The next day at work, Forrest asked Ken and me to have lunch with him because he wanted to discuss something he had heard on the golf course. Once we were seated Forrest confronted Ken and I about the scathing emails that were sent to the builder concerning the house. He said that the builder had told people at the club that he had never had so much trouble with a client before. Ken immediately got defensive and said that the builder and the foreman were terrible and that everything written in the emails were true. Then he told Forrest that I had drafted the letter and that he thought the tone was a little harsh as well, but that I was very angry and that my mother agreed with me.

I almost fell out of my chair! I had never seen Ken lie so easily. He made it sound so believable; the lies just flowed out of his mouth. There was not even a hint of truth to any of it. I had not even seen the email.

Forrest said that before we put anything in writing we need to be sure of what we are doing. He said we must not attack people in the community and put the Burnett name on it because it reflected badly on him. Forrest directed his comments to me since Ken had blamed me for the incident.

When Ken and I went back to work, he acted as if nothing had happened. I could not believe how he could separate himself like that. We did not even discuss it. I am slowly becoming a doormat wife.

I felt mentally drained after what happened, so I used the excuse that I needed to check on Logan and went home. When I got there, Logan had just finished an episode where he had locked himself in Ken's office and used a paperweight to bang on the door. Vera was worried that Ken was going to be angry with her about the marks Logan had left on the door. I told Vera to go home and noticed how spent she looked despite her muscular, six-foot-tall frame.

Mom made dinner and was feeding the kids when Ken got home. He did his usual hugging and kissing the kids, showering them with affection. My mother had been there long enough to notice that Ken never hugged me when he got home. The kids went to the playroom after eating while we had our dinner. Then Ken went out again to attend the Home Owner's Association Board meeting.

I told my mom that I felt like something was up with Ken. Little did I know that the drama about to unfold would turn my life completely inside out. Mom told me that she had read a quote somewhere that said, "Spend your time on those people who love you unconditionally and don't waste it on those who only love you when the conditions are right for them." That comment really made me think. Then Mom said very gently, "I don't like the way he treats you Kate, he doesn't even hug you or speak to you when he comes home." I told her that I didn't know what to do. Ken and I disagree about Logan's care and he blamed me for the bad behavior. Ken would not accept that Logan had a medical condition so he refused to deal with it. My life was not how she imagined it. Mom had concern in her eyes.

Ken was nice to me when people were around, which made me want to always have company. I dreaded being alone with him because he was so critical of me. Mom took me in her arms and held me for a long time. Then she said, "I am always here for you baby; you just have to make the best of it for Emma." Mom encouraged me to spend time with my girlfriends and take care of myself.

My mother's visit came to end and now I had to decide what to do about Logan. Wearily I made an appointment with the head of the best child and adolescent psychiatrist for a complete evaluation. It was time to bring in the big guns.

T.T. Johnson

Chapter 13

Ken found it very difficult to deal with the reality that we had a specialist treating Logan for mental and behavioral disorders. To get his thoughts in order, he decided that he needed a break so he arranged to attend a nine-day conference in California. He had already booked the flight and hotel when he informed me that he was going. Nevertheless, I agreed that it would be good for him to go and thought he might bring home some good ideas from the conference. Actually, I needed a break from him as well. Absence makes the heart grow fonder; right?

One night when Ken was away, I was startled awake by Logan who was standing next to my bed. He was nude and had taken a blue sharpie marker and colored his skin. It had to have taken him hours to get that amount of coverage over his chest and genitals. He had colored a mask on his face and one blue sleeve down his arm. This gave any tattoo artist a run for their money. I said, "Holy crap, Batman... what have you done?" Logan had one leg completely colored royal blue and the top of both feet. I looked on the bottom of his feet to see if blue sharpie foot prints were going to be all over the freaking house. Thank goodness, the bottoms of his feet were not colored blue. I took pictures of him because it was hysterical and we were both laughing at his new look. He was so proud of what he had done.

I ran bath water not knowing what else to do at 3 AM and put bubbles in it. I pointed to the tub and said, "To the bat cave Batman" and then put on a bathing suit and kneeled beside the tub after Logan got in. The marker was dry and Logan was "permanently" a super hero tatted up by his own hand. He had half his chest colored and was in a very good mood. There was no getting the marker off and it had stained Logan light skin and then I noticed his hair. Logan had colored his light hair above his ear like a fender over a wheel. I laughed long and hard and Logan giggled with me. Logan would place his Hulk Action figure on the side of the tub and I would say, "You talking to me! NO!" and push it into the bubbles. Logan put Hulk back on the edge of the tub again and again. He would cackle with laughter eyes shut mouth open. This was a story that I would tell over and over again. It was a fun time with Logan that we both needed. He stayed in the tub until the water got cold and then we drained some and added more.

I was tired of constantly experiencing fear it was nice to have times like this one with Logan. Emma squealed with laughter the next morning when Logan showed off his new blue super hero costume. All the ink was still there and I don't think gasoline would have even removed it. It was just going to have to wear off. Logan could not have been more pleased that the ink was here to stay.

Emma kept her door locked at night because I did not feel she was safe. Logan did not know how to properly handle his emotions. It seemed to excite him to see my fear and he would laugh at me. It was hard to parent a violent, abusive, uncontrollable, hyperactive child. I loved him and feared him at the same time. I had learned to hide my emotions from Logan in order to protect myself.

The next day was Saturday and Emma had a birthday party to attend. After dropping her off, Logan and I were on the way home and he was playing a handheld game. I parked the car but Logan refused to get out of the car because he was not finished with the game, so I left him there. As I walked away, I looked back and saw him punching and kicking the seats. I went back and opened all the car doors and then the chase began. He jumped from front seat to back seat as I tried to catch him by the arm or grab his shirt. When I finally grabbed his shirt, he took it off. I was afraid he would take off running because he was a fast runner and hard to catch. Logan is still colored blue and looks ridiculous. He refused to be called Logan and said he was Batman not Logan. So I said, "Batman get out of the car."

Finally I was able to take hold of his upper arm and stood him outside by the car. He began playing with his handheld game again as I locked the car, and then suddenly, as if a switch were flipped, he climbed up on the roof of the car and started jumping on it like a trampoline. He would slam his butt down then stand up, jump down, stand up, jump down until the roof was dented and had started to cave-in. I screamed at him to stop, but he wouldn't. As the entire roof began to bow and cave in, I reached for my cell phone and called my friend, Maggie.

Maggie called her husband Mark, who was six-foot-five, two-hundred-and-five pounds, to come help. He got on one side of the car and I got on the other. Mark caught Logan by the foot then was able to grab him underneath his armpits. I grabbed him by his feet and we carried him as he screamed and kicked all the way up to the house. He managed to bite Mark on the hand and arm so Mark flipped him over his shoulder, but Logan continued to bite Mark on the back and pound him with his fists.

Once we got inside the front door Mark released Logan, but Logan ran and grabbed a bar stool and started swinging it as a weapon. Then he threw the bar stool and it landed near the large plate-glass wall. Mark grabbed him again and pinned him down while I ran to get a sedative that would dissolve in his mouth. We had to get him calmed down. As I placed the tablet in his open mouth he was yelling, biting and spitting at me. Finally, with Mark by my side helping me hold him, I was able to place Logan in a protective hold that the doctor had suggested I use.

Logan's breathing finally started to slow down so I sat him up and we backed away. Instantly he went for his next weapon, grabbing my coin bag he began throwing change at me. Mark yelled, "What do I do?" By then Logan was hitting me with the silk bag and it stung my leg. Mark took the coin bag away, which agitated Logan even more so he wrapped his hand in my hair and pulled me to the ground. I was pinned to the floor by a six-year-old boy! In our struggle, Logan kicked me in the ribs and pain seared through my body. Mark and I were able to put Logan into a protective hold, trying to keep him from hurting himself or one of us.

All three of us were covered in sweat when Mark pulled Logan off of me. I went limp with exhaustion and once again, Logan "flipped a switch" and started playing with his game-boy. I thanked Mark and told him that everything was OK now and that Logan had experienced worse episodes in the past.

Horrified, Mark looked at me and said, "You cannot handle this child. I'm a large guy and he was difficult for me. This isn't going to work and why the hell is he colored blue?"

At that moment, reality began to set in. Mark was right. I could not keep doing this. Eventually, Logan was going to hurt me. I don't know what I would have done if Emma had been there.

Vera came over to spend a few nights and I told her that I would pay her whatever she wanted if she would stay with me until Ken got back. I did not want to be alone with Logan. Vera had giant hands and handled Logan better than I could. She was a godsend and I could not have done this without her.

"Do you want me to check his head for three sixes?" Vera asked.

I sarcastically smiled and shook my head, but must admit that I wondered at times. It seemed that Logan's behavior was getting more bizarre and more violent with each passing day.

After calming down some, I called Ken in California and told him what had happened. I really wanted him to leave the conference and come home, but he said that he would have to call Mark to see if it was as bad as I made it seem.

Ken called me back in an hour and told me that he decided not to come home. Then he instructed me to call Logan's behavioral counselor and tell her what had happened. I called Pam and set up an emergency session for the next day.

Pam came to the house the next morning with plans to observe him for a full day. We went over his medication schedule and his daily routine, as Pam wanted to know what Vera and Logan did each day. After some basic updating, she settled in and began to observe him in the playroom.

After dropping Emma off at school, I met JoAnne at the Drip-O-Lator for coffee and began to unpack for her the last episode with Logan. After hearing what had happened she said, "That is not normal behavior, no one acts like that. Was his birthmother on drugs or mentally ill?"

The Shattered Faberge Egg

I told JoAnne that I had wondered the same thing. Then she asked if we had considered whether Logan could have Asperger Syndrome. I said that I had read everything I could find on it and didn't think that was it. I explained that we were told by the adoption agency that Logan was healthy, but clearly something was wrong. JoAnne said she was very worried about me and afraid that someone was going to get hurt. I did not tell her that Logan had kicked me in the ribs so hard that it knocked the breath out of me. I was humiliated that my adopted son could act so horrible.

Too quickly our time together came to a close, so I gave JoAnne a hug and told her that I had to get back home since Pam was there observing Logan. When I arrived, Logan was screaming and had broken a vase by smashing it on the master bedroom door. "Here we go again" I thought.

Vera gave me quick rundown of what had taken place. Waving her giant hands in the air she said, "Logan threw a glass of orange juice on the floor because he didn't want to eat at the table and then he threw a framed picture. Pam has tried to calm him using different techniques."

Logan ran by screaming so I grabbed him. I was trying to hold him when he bit my hand, pinched me on the arm, and began to hit me. Pam told me to begin placing him in a hold, but Logan broke free of my grip and locked himself in the bathroom. He began slamming the toilet seat over and over while screaming, "I hate you." He was already hoarse because he had been screaming for so long.

There was a decorative wooden box on the back of the toilet that Logan grabbed and threw it against the glass shower door. Then he threw it against the back of the bathroom door.

Vera had called the doctor who said, "Give him double the Risperdal and a Klonopin, and take him to the ER if he doesn't calm down soon." I emphasized that there was no way we could get him in a car and drive because I was afraid that he would hurt us all. The doctor said to call 911 if necessary.

I kept talking to Logan after hanging up with the doctor because it had grown very quiet in the bathroom. Vera tried to pick the lock, but

Logan was holding the button in, a trick he had already learned. He was very smart.

Finally, Logan mumbled, "Mommy, I'm thirsty" and came out of the bathroom wanting me to hold him. He was very loving and hugged my neck. He had gone from a feral animal to a very loving child after a thirty-five-minute tantrum.

Vera brought Logan some juice and I just sat holding him. Pam said she would come back the next day, so I told her that around six p.m. was the "witching hour" when Logan became the worst.

When Pam arrived the next evening, Logan was in a foul mood. I turned off the television and Logan became angry, pinching my face. Then he spit on me and said, "Turn it on." I put him in a hold and he bit both of my hands, one so hard that a blood-blister instantly appeared. Logan was seated in front of me and I had my arms wrapped around him. I yelled at Emma to go up to her room and then Logan lunged backwards and used the back of his head to head-butt me. The blow hurt and brought tears to my eyes. He said, "I don't like you." Pam came close and told Logan that I would let him go if he calmed down. Logan spit on her and was able to get one arm loose and smacked her in the face knocking off her glasses. He responded by laughing.

After about ten minutes Logan calmed down and I was able to release him. He said that he wanted to watch TV so Pam told him he could. Pam and I took this opportunity for her to read over my journals regarding Logan's behavior. Hearing her read aloud what I had written sounded unreal:

Monday, April 8: Logan hit Emma and tried to bite her. Tried to knock her down when she was putting on her rollerblades. Then was very sweet and loving and played with her.

Tuesday, April 9: Logan is very afraid to sleep in his room he thinks there are bugs in his air vents. I am very worried about him. I worry about the future and if he will kill me in the night sometime. I do love him very much and want him to be okay. I also think about using an apartment over the garage for the nanny so that Logan can stay with her two nights a week so I can sleep.

The Shattered Faberge Egg

Wednesday, April 10: Logan threw orange juice on Emma's school books and said, "I don't like you, stupid. I hate you." He slammed doors and broke his Spiderman fishing pole in half. He spit at me and turned over the leather chair. He would not stop running and was doing laps around the house.

Thursday, April 11: Logan was agitated and kept saying "I need to hit someone." He said there were lizards in his room and wanted me to check under the bed. I looked under the bed and there were 5 red solo cups filled with urine all lined up in a row.

Friday, April 12: Logan says there are bugs in his room again in his air vents. Threw bowl of ice cream across the room and shattered the dish because I did not give him enough.

Pam asked me if I had documented everything. I told her that I didn't have time and only put down one episode a day. It was hard enough to do that.

Pam said, "He is violent and I am concerned with his antisocial behavior, frequent loss of temper and his tantrums. I am most concerned about his cruelty toward the dog." Pam explained that as she was observing Logan watching TV, Skipper our dog, was lying next to Logan when he reached over and pulled his paw apart until Skipper cried out in pain. Then Logan grabbed Skipper, held him down, and sat on him until the dog peed on the floor in fear.

I was stunned and felt terrible for our little King Charles Cavalier Spaniel. Ken paid $2400 for this puppy. The dog was so sweet and gentle. Now I had to keep the dog safe from Logan too. This was too much. There was more going on here than I could see. I asked Pam what was wrong with Logan and she said, "It is too early to tell, but I have seen children like this before. Usually it was because their birthmothers used drugs while they were pregnant." She went on to say, "Logan is young, and most psychiatrists will not issue a diagnosis until he is in his teens. With his destructive, dangerous and violent behavior, we should prepare for it to get worse as he gets bigger." She also said that we needed to find a good home for Skipper immediately.

Pam contacted Ken in California to update him about the dog since I was already calling friends whom I thought would be able to help.

When I called my friend, Belinda, and asked her if she still wanted a "King Charles" she said she would love to have him. Everyone wanted one in our neighborhood. When Emma and I drove Skipper over to Belinda's she hugged Emma and told her that she could come over anytime to see him. On our way home I told Emma how sorry I was about Skipper. That was when she told me that Logan had choked him a few days before. She said that she felt sorry for him. Emma was already an old soul. She knew that Logan was very sick and she also knew that I was on my last leg.

Ken returned from California and quickly realized that I needed a break. He said, "I don't know what to do about Logan. Let's you and I take a short trip to see if we can sort it out. Emma can stay with Jill and the twins and Vera can stay here with Logan. He does better when he's one-on-one and nobody else is here." I agreed. It was true that Logan did better when others were not around. Ken said that we could go to the Kentucky Derby because I had always wanted to. He also suggested that we invite Mark and Maggie and make a weekend trip out of it. Ken wanted to do something nice for Mark since he had helped me with Logan's fit.

Though weary, I was relieved that Ken may finally be facing the fact that Logan was beyond our reach. It was obvious that he was struggling with mental illness and we were not equipped to handle it.

Chapter 14

To get ready for our weekend get-away, Maggie and I went out and bought large hats with bows on them and had a great time trying them all on. It was very stress relieving to shop for what I hoped would be a fun weekend with friends at the Kentucky Derby.

Ken told Vera that he would trade in her van for a new car if she would watch Logan for the weekend. She was driving an older model and needed a newer, safer vehicle. Vera took Ken up on the offer so he had the dealership drive over a new car. In reality, Ken was just tired of looking at that old van in the driveway. We arranged for Emma to stay with her Aunt Jill while we were gone.

We flew business class to Louisville and went straight to the Galt House Hotel. All of the rooms were booked but Ken managed to get us two suites with waterfront balconies. The Galt house is the largest hotel In Kentucky and the official Derby hotel.

After settling in, we went to the hotel conservatory, an impressive glass-domed room modeled after the Crystal Palace in London. There were tropical plants all around and birds inside the dome. For more than an hour we sat and ate appetizers, talking about our "bucket lists." The Kentucky Derby was on my list, and I was anxious to hear what Mark and Maggie had on theirs.

Mark was in Alcoholics Anonymous and had been doing very well, so Maggie and I ordered sweet tea to keep him from feeling uncomfortable. Ken had a glass of wine, and Mark assured us that it was fine for us to get a drink if we wanted one. Ken was being nice to me that day and I was happy and feeling good.

I told everyone I wanted to charter a yacht and cruise the Italian Rivera; Maggie said she wanted to learn how to make stained glass. I started laughing and said, "No way, stained glass?" Ken had left the table for a few minutes and then came back all excited. He had managed to get tickets to THE Kentucky Derby Party. The tickets were $1,650 per person and all the celebrities would be there so we just had to attend.

    The hotel arranged for a driver to drop us off. I felt very special. We saw Serena Williams, Eli and Peyton Manning, Faith Hill and Tim McGraw. There were so many people attending it was hard to find a place to sit. Everything was very elegant since it was a black tie affair. It had been a long time since I was able to relax and enjoy myself with Ken. He was so much fun when other people were around and he was in charge of the plans.

    On Saturday, we made our way to Church Hill Downs and found our seats in the Turf Club. We arrived early enough to go down to the track to walk on the hallowed ground and take a few pictures.

    After walking the track we went to the paddock, which was packed full of horse racing fans, each one trying to look at the horses and their jockeys. Maggie and I were taken with the beautiful red roses in bloom everywhere and the gorgeous landscaping. It was a great place for watching people. We saw pretty women dressed to the nines and old guys in wacky pants and glorious hats. Maggie commented on how it was totally a "Ken move" in how he had set us up. Ken always said, "Go big or go home" and he had done that for sure.

    Next we went to the betting windows and placed our bets. Maggie and I had picked our horses by their name and the color of the jockeys' clothing. Our seats were great and we had private restrooms, which were very nice. We went up to the sky terrace to see if we could catch a glimpse of another celebrity. Ken ordered a Mint Julep, which I thought was totally nasty; Maggie said it tasted like mouthwash. Then the trumpets began to sound. We didn't care who won or who was up for the Triple Crown, we just wanted to have fun placing our bets.

    We had a table for four at the "members only" Turf Club. It was race time, and after the singing of "My Old Kentucky Home" the race began. The horses took off like lightening and the noise from the crowd was deafening. Maggie's horse pulled out in front so she was screaming, "That's my horse, that's my horse!" but another horse won in the final seconds. It was a blast and for us was the greatest two minutes ever in sports.

Our time away ended way too soon. As our plane was landing back home I began feeling anxious. We were back to reality and I wondered how Logan had behaved. Vera reported that he'd had a good weekend and just played Xbox games the whole time. I was relieved.

Joanne's birthday arrived so we decided to go to the spa after Emma went to school. We wrapped ourselves in plush robes, drank tea, and ate little cups of yogurt-dipped fruit while waiting for our treatments. JoAnne picked out the white chocolate chips and gave them to me because she knew how much I loved them.

Joanne asked me how Ken was dealing with the fact that Logan was not "normal." I told her that he was not dealing with it at all. I told her that Ken always had a diversion tactic because he liked everything to be a surprise. He always had to one-up everyone else, so we didn't even send Christmas cards. Instead, we sent Happy New Year cards so that ours would stand out from the others. JoAnne said she loved our cards and that she really liked the one where we were in the hot air balloon and the one where we were under-water.

"Most people put a picture of the family at the beach or Disney World on the card, but yours is at Disney World from inside Cinderella's Coach. Who does that?" Joanne said.

"Ken does" I said. "He will do whatever it takes to show off."

I reminded JoAnne that the first year Ken and I were married he found out I liked to listen to Johann Sebastian Bach. Most men would buy their wife a CD or load her phone with the music of Bach. Not Ken. He flew me to Leipzig, Germany, and took me to St. Thomas Church where Bach was the choirmaster. There was even a museum in the church dedicated to him.

JoAnne said that after church the previous Sunday everyone was talking at lunch about our trip to the Kentucky Derby and wondered what Ken had done. He had a lot of time on his hands and this afforded him the ability to plan these excursions. He was always on his laptop in his office at home and would not let me in. He also would not allow me to pick up the mail. Ken was very private about his phone and his computer and said it was so I would not spoil any of his surprises.

By that time our pedicures were dry and I had to pick up Emma, so I hugged JoAnne goodbye and we parted. I noticed that I had missed a call from Vera. Little did I know how that call was going to change my life.

When Emma and I arrived home Logan was in a full-blown manic attack. Vera had called Ken for help but couldn't reach him, so she called Maureen.

Ken had told Vera to stop all of Logan's medications while we were away at the Derby, and the detox had caused him to have a psychotic break. He was in constant motion, running around and saying "liddle, liddle, liddle" and other nonsensical words.

Logan tried to rip Maureen's necklace off and then he put his hands around her neck to choke her. Vera pulled him off, but he was able to wiggle free and began hitting his own arm yelling that he was going to break it. Maureen grabbed her cell phone, called 911, and told them that we had an emergency and needed an ambulance.

Breathlessly, Vera said, "Ken made me take him off all meds. He was sure it was the meds making him act badly, that it was all side effects." Things start to go in slow motion for me.

I started to panic. It was plain to me that Logan was highly agitated and his behavior was more erratic than usual. I ordered Emma to go to her room, lock the door and put on her headphones.

Logan ran into the bathroom and slammed the door. When Ken finally walked in, Maureen tried to update him about the fit, but she was nearly hysterical as she told him what had happened: "Locked bathroom door; throws back toilet lid cover to tile floor and breaks it in half; punches holes in dry wall; choked me and punched Vera in the behind so hard it will bruise. Logan is a walking stick of dynamite. Very loud screaming. Threw hand-held weight across room. Scratching, punching, yelling, biting, then ran to bathroom again. Broke toilet paper roll off wall; broke toilet lid in half."

Maureen had never witnessed one of Logan's full-blown episodes, and certainly had never experienced being beaten by him. She had never seen how he tore up the house, nor experienced how hard he was to handle.

Finally, the ambulance arrived. Logan was biting, spitting and hitting the paramedics so they strapped him on a backboard and gave him a shot to sedate him. It was hard to believe that this was a seven-year-old boy!

Vera was still very shaken and was rambling, "One minute sweet and loving then it was like a switch was flipped and Logan would attack. Then it would turn off again."

Ken and I followed the ambulance to the hospital in his car. Logan was admitted. He was transferred to Atlanta and spent two weeks as an inpatient in the psychiatric ward at Peachtree Hospital. When he threatened to jump out of the window, they put him in a specialized treatment unit for children. There the doctors diagnosed him with schizophrenia.

We began to search for Logan's birthmother and family in order to gain some insight into what may be contributing to his behavior. Ken located the grandparents in River Ridge, Louisiana, and demanded information about the birthmother, Lisa. Ken explained that Logan was sick and we needed medical information immediately. The grandmother stated that Lisa had come to live with them when she was sixteen because her mother was insane. She had lived with them for two years and became pregnant when she turned seventeen. He learned that she used drugs and drank alcohol during her pregnancy. She did not want the baby, but it was too late for her to have an abortion.

Ken asked Lisa's grandmother if a doctor had formally diagnosed Lisa's mother and asked where she was living. Lisa's grandmother told Ken that Lisa's mom was homeless and wandered the streets. She said she was schizophrenic and refused to take medication.

Ken was furious. He said that we would have never adopted Logan had we known the truth because schizophrenia is hereditary. The grandmother cried and said she prayed that Logan would not have the same thing. Then she said he cried all the time as a newborn and didn't sleep for more than four hours at a time. She said they were unable to care for Lisa and Logan so they placed him up for adoption.

As Ken told me what he had learned, I became sick and angry. Now more than ever we were unsure of what the future held. This problem was bigger than we ever expected and we had no idea what to do moving forward. I was frightened for Emma and for myself. What were we going to do?

Evelyn wanted Logan to go to the Boston's Children hospital where they had expert child psychiatrists, so Ken and his parents made plans to go. I stayed home to be with Emma, which also gave Vera some much needed time off.

Logan was admitted to the Behavioral Center and was placed on a ward with other children who also had early-onset schizophrenia. He fit the criteria for family history (drug use during pregnancy), visual hallucinations of objects that were not there, and violent damaging behavior (he told a nurse, "I will cut you with a knife").

All of the pieces were finally coming together after hearing what the doctors told us. Logan talked and laughed to himself and shut out real people and surroundings. It was as if he were in his own little world all closed off from us.

Logan felt as if someone was spying on him in the hospital and felt threatened by staying there. He was extremely irritable, had rapid fluctuating moods and daily had angry outbursts in the unit. He had always "made up words" and had his own language. We thought it was just him being a little boy, not part of some psychosis. Logan often demonstrated regressive behavior by suddenly acting much younger than his current age and being clingy, wanting to be carried everywhere. At times he would scream at the TV to "shut up." Logan's behavior was starting to make more sense to me as I studied his symptoms.

Schizophrenia explained his extreme moodiness, irritability and why he easily became confused and agitated. It also explained his outbursts that came from nowhere simply because he did not like a noise in a room. The psychiatrists felt his birthmother's drug use during pregnancy played a part in his rage attacks; it also explained why his teeth were stained brownish yellow.

The staff evaluated Logan for two more weeks and reported that they felt he needed to have a full-time, live-in caregiver (handler) to watch him at all times. The psychiatrist explained that Logan acted in a frenzied rage with amazing strength, which was why he was so hard for me to handle. He was prone to violence and when he got "amped up" on adrenaline, the floodgates of anxiety opened and he failed to notice that he was hurting others. He just needed to be in control and had no remorse for causing pain or injury.

Ken and I agreed to take Logan back home after the team of doctor's carefully monitored different medications used for controlling schizophrenia. Needless to say, our future looked and felt very bleak.

Our dreams of having a loving, healthy little boy were dashed. Fear and dread had replaced the anticipation and excitement of parenting this beautiful child. Our lives had turned into a living nightmare. Welcome to the Island of Misfit Toys.

T.T. Johnson

Chapter 15

After Logan was released from the hospital we hired an orderly named Thomas to help us. He was with us during the day and Vera was with us at night.

Logan had a very rough reentry coming home. Over the first few days he broke a dining room chair, threw the Sony Play Station, punched Emma in the stomach, pinched me on the arm and kicked me on the shin. One day during an hour long rage, he repeatedly said, "I hate you." He was uncontrollable; up at midnight, 2:00 a.m., 4:00 a.m., and 4:30 a.m. One night he walked into our room saying he wanted a milkshake, and then he asked why it was so dark.

Emma was under tremendous stress by this time and I was worried about her. Logan was bothersome and hyper, and was not very nice to her. When he got angry with her, he would pee in her dresser drawer.

At night, Logan would get up and do destructive things. One night, he took Liquid Paper white-out and painted the back of Ken's dark mahogany office door. His moods cycled in and out and he was wild and loud, making it very difficult to be around him. Some nights we were awakened to blood curdling screams; every day was a struggle.

Logan was on so many drugs it was ridiculous. He was on Risperdal, Concerta, Tripeptal, and Klonopin. Occasionally he had a look of hatred in his eyes that chilled me to the bone, while at other times he was loving and kind.

One night Logan was up at 3:00 a.m. and could not go back to sleep. Vera was up with him and put a Veggie Tales movie in for him to watch, but he was very loud and everyone in the house woke up.

When I went to check on Vera, I picked up Logan and he spit in my hair. Then he began screaming and ran into the garage and grabbed a hand-held weight and threw it at the door. Vera gave him a juice box to get him to come back in and watch TV, but as I turned around to walk inside Logan hit me square in the back with the corner of the juice box. I moaned in pain and he laughed, and then he scratched Vera and called her a butthead. Next he gritted his teeth and gave out a loud guttural yell.

Thomas didn't last very long. He quit saying he had never had a patient who was this agitated. Out of concern for Emma's safety, the psychiatrist office referred Nayda Parker, a social worker, to evaluate Logan.

When Nayda arrived, she said that she wanted to observe Logan eating dinner. I explained to her that he would not sit at the table to eat so he ate in front of the TV. That evening Logan had asked for macaroni and cheese so I made him a bowl and he watched the movie "Cars" while he ate.

Nayda questioned me about Logan's daily activities, so I explained that we had to watch him every minute or he got into things. I told her how he had taken a magic marker in the middle of the night and completely colored his penis blue.

When Logan finished his dinner, Nayda said she wanted to see his bath and bedtime routine. I asked her if she was sure because she had no idea what she was getting into. She told me that she was there to make sure that we could provide basic care to Logan and still protect Emma.

That evening, Ken and Emma were out shopping and Vera was off since two adults were in the home. I went into the bathroom and ran Logan's bathwater and then told him that it was time to take a bath. He walked into the bathroom and said he didn't want to wash his hair. I told him that we were going to wash his hair and he became angry. He got in the tub and immediately began to kick and splash water all over the bathroom. I yelled at him to stop, but he refused and kept it up for fifteen minutes. By the time he stopped, I was soaking wet, my makeup was running down my face and water was all over the floor.

Nayda's eyes were wide with disbelief when she said, "Take hold of his upper arm and pull him out. I am afraid he will hurt himself in the tub."

The Shattered Faberge Egg

I did exactly as she said and pulled Logan out of the tub dripping wet. As I turned to get a towel he grabbed my hair, wrapped it around his hand and made a fist. Then he yanked me by the hair and pinned my head to the floor. It was a full-on brawl so I screamed for Nayda to help. She refused saying that she was not allowed to touch a child.

My head was flat on the tile floor and I was in tears from the pain of Logan pulling my hair. He was standing over me when he suddenly bit me on the arm. Struggling with Logan, I jerked my arm away to get him off me and my arm hit him right in the testicles. When he let go of my hair I jumped to my feet and saw him standing there with a long clump of my hair in his hand. I quickly wrapped him in a towel, picked him up and put him in front of the TV still holding the long strand of hair. I told Nayda that he had never grabbed my hair like that. She noticed blood coming from my scalp and got a paper towel to press into the wound.

Nayda asked me if bath time was always this hard. I told her that he splashed like that every time. She said that she needed to call her supervisor and stepped outside on the front porch. I checked on Logan and then changed into a dry shirt. I twisted my wet hair up in a clip and wiped the black streaks of mascara off my face. My scalp was very sore, and there was a blood blister on my arm where he bit me.

Nayda came back in and said, "I checked with my supervisor and I don't have to report this as sexual abuse."

I was instantly angered and asked Nayda what she was talking about.

"It was an accident that you hit him in the testicles." Nayda said.

"I would never abuse my child. He was hurting me. You witnessed the whole incident." I said.

Nayda said, "I am just doing my job. I have never experienced anything like this."

At that point, Logan walked in with a box of Kleenex, handed one to me, climbed up on my lap, and hugged me affectionately.

Nayda continued taking notes and then told me that she would write a report and send it to Logan's psychiatrist. She also told me to take Logan to see the doctor the next morning. Ken and Emma came in as

Nayda was leaving so she gave Ken a quick report while I took Emma upstairs to bed.

When we took Logan to see the psychiatrist back in Atlanta, he determined that we needed to put him back in the hospital. After Logan had been there a week, his team of doctors called a conference to discuss his illness. The lead psychiatrist asked if we wanted to bring any other family members with us for support, which was the first sign that they were going to deliver bad news. Ken called Forest and Maureen and asked them to be there with us. Mom was in Charleston and Jill had the twins.

We were seated around a big conference table when a flock of white coats filed in. Dr. Minton began the conversation saying, "We have spent the last week evaluating Logan and monitoring his behavior, and believe that we have reached a formal diagnosis with some new information we have gathered."

Everyone leaned in and listened very intently as Dr. Minton continued… "Logan appears to be exhibiting classic symptoms of schizophrenia. Many patients diagnosed with this are not this violent, however the substance abuse of the birth-mother is a contributing factor that worsens the symptoms and causes violent behavior. The psychotherapists working with Logan have identified that Logan has a main hallucination named "Owen." Logan constantly sees Owen and he hears Owen tell him to be violent to others."

We were shocked and dismayed at the news. It was still soaking in as Dr. Minton went on to say: "After evaluating Logan's actions during this hospital stay, and observing continued signs of disturbance, we are very concerned. His threats to harm himself and others must be taken seriously. Just today, Logan told me again that he was going to jump out of the window and kill himself."

I could see that Ken was startled by this statement. Then Forest asked, "What is the treatment plan to handle this?"

Dr. Minton replied, "Logan was an early starter and with his childhood onset and anti-social behavior we have to take into consideration that there is an elevated risk for Logan to engage in violence toward others. He has repeatedly engaged in aggressive behavior toward his care givers.

"Logan's inappropriate laughter and unpredictable behavior is due to the schizophrenia. The out-of-control behavior and irritability is likely due to the birth mother exposing him to drug abuse in the womb. We can't be one-hundred percent positive due to Logan's age, but we can be sure that Logan has a dual diagnosis with fetal drug exposure and schizophrenia."

I was listening very intently and felt that the doctor was hedging and had more to say.

Dr. Minton continued: "The fetal drug damage compromises Logan's quality of life and requires ongoing treatment...for his lifetime. As a family, you need to take into consideration that it is dangerous for Emma since she is so young. The risk of Emma being injured by Logan due to his mental illness is high. Violence in the home environment by any family member can lead to chronic instability, but Logan's chaotic lifestyle and your family's disharmony could cause Emma's development to become seriously compromised."

Ken spoke up, "What are you trying to say Doctor?"

"Logan has been admitted more than once to psychiatric wards and as he grows older his impairment and lack of control will become more serious. The risk of violence is elevated and Logan could end up assaulting and killing those who care for him. I am sorry for the huge amount of suffering that your family has been through. The multiple risk factors lead the team to recommend permanent placement in a locked residential treatment facility." Dr. Minton replied.

Ken said, "Are you serious?" Maureen let out a huge sigh and began to cry. I was not breathing. Ken argued, "You mean right now? He is seven-years old!"

Dr. Minton paused so this could sink in. "It is not your fault that something is wrong with Logan's brain. He is on the border of this world and his world. His medication has been changed to Tegretol, Thorazine and Lithium. We hope this will blunt some of the rage.

"Child-onset schizophrenia is twenty to thirty times more severe than adult-onset. Ninety-five percent of the time when Logan is awake he is actively hallucinating. I have never seen a child this sick in all the years I have been practicing."

I asked if I could see him. I wanted to whisper in his ear, "Mommy loves you" like I did every night.

"Yes, but I want to prepare you for what happened last night. Logan had a tantrum that escalated and he slammed his head into the floor, resulting in a gash that required a few sutures. He had a rough day today, he hit the therapy dog and we restrain a patient if they are becoming aggressive, so we placed him in restraints on his bed. This sent him over the edge so it was necessary to sedate him. His new medications have not had time to fully take effect."

Everyone at the table was quiet. Dr. Minton said, "Logan is among the rarest of rare: a violent schizophrenic child. I fear you are not safe and want you to consider the options I have suggested. It won't be easy finding a place for him as there are not many treatment centers of this type. I have already contacted two residential facilities and was rejected because they are at full census."

Dr. Posada said, "This ward is not designed for long-term care and we need to decide where Logan will discharge once his new meds are stable."

I was numb. I felt as if all of the air had been sucked out of the room and I couldn't breathe. Ken's eyes were fixed in a vacant stare as he tried to comprehend everything that we had just been told. Forrest was holding Maureen as she quietly sobbed on his shoulder.

Chapter 16

Against medical advice, Ken demanded that we bring Logan home so we could keep him under our watchful care. As he promised, Ken became a part of Logan's care team and was very involved. My primary goal was keeping Emma safe. Besides, I was flat-out afraid of Logan and believed the doctor's recommendations were just.

We moved Logan into Vera's apartment over the garage and she moved into the guest room in the main house, which made it simpler for us to take shifts with Logan. The second night Ken was with Logan, he left the key out on the table. Seizing the opportunity, Logan took the key and escaped from the apartment. Once outside, he ran down the street in and out of traffic with Ken chasing after him. I wondered then how much more it would take before Ken gave in. I guess he needed to experience some episodes like Vera and I had before he would consent to placing Logan in a residential treatment home.

Logan had morbid hallucinations of Owen pushing him to do daring nightmarish stunts. It was horrendous! We had a child that we had raised and loved very much, but it was not safe to be with him. We had been through anguish with Logan and suffered much tragedy. Looking back it is hard to imagine what we went through. He lived in a very different reality.

Watching Logan talk to Owen sent chills up my spine. He saw shadows that were not there and was completely irrational. He would scream, "I want to hit her, I want to hit her" and was in a constant state of paranoia. With each passing day he digressed more and more. He accused Emma of hiding his toys and taking his things so we stopped bringing him into the main house or near Emma except once a day for a special visit.

Logan hated the dark and wanted all the lights on so he would get up at night and go through the apartment turning on all the lights. He had hallucinations and saw bugs and lizards everywhere. Owen liked to draw blood; he was a hallucination that represented pure evil. He would tell Logan to lure me into the room so he could ambush me or smash my face with the TV remote. One day I asked Logan what he was hearing and he said, "Owen wants a hammer or a rock to hit with." We were all afraid of Owen, even Logan.

Logan put me thru hell on my nights in the apartment. I was afraid that he would escape and sneak into the main house, so I hid the key to the deadbolt and locked myself in the second bedroom. One night Logan came to my door and said, "We want a knife. We are going to stab you when you go to sleep." His destructive, problematic behavior created panic situations in our house. As a mother, I was tortured by his violent reactions when there was no explanation for them.

One of my journal entries reads:

Frightened… behavior getting more aggressive….we can't take care of Logan.

Behavior disturbs me. Owen and lizards are what Logan sees continually. Logan says "WE will hit you" or "WE will hurt you." Very impulsive. Sleep is off again. Pooped on the floor. Biting, screaming, threw hot coffee on Ken when we were changing shifts. I want to do the right thing for Logan, but I don't feel like doing this anymore.

The most difficult part was how Logan lashed out at those who loved him and were desperately trying to help him. In the end, he drove everyone away. We were all frustrated and I desperately wanted a normal life for Emma.

Ken was at the breaking point. It was difficult for him to cope with the possible loss of his child. Death almost seemed easier than locking Logan away. His life ahead seemed bleak and his hallucinations were of a person who was a cold-blooded killer. Crying, Ken told his mom over the phone, "It is so bad."

Not feeling guilty about wanting Logan to go was very difficult because he tormented our family. Emma's personal safety was a

The Shattered Faberge Egg

priority, but Ken still allowed Logan to see her once a day. Logan was upset so he climbed up the outside of the staircase and then turned on Emma with hatred burning in his eyes. A sense of terror came over Ken as it dawned on him that Logan was about to attack. Then Logan launched himself off the staircase with his fist in the air and jumped on Emma's back. She fell flat out on the travertine floor while Logan continued punching her, delivering multiple blows.

When Ken was able to pull Logan off Emma he saw that her mouth was bloody from biting her lip when she hit the floor. She was crying so I carried her into the kitchen to check her for injuries. I took a dishcloth and applied pressure to her lip to stop the bleeding and then pulled her head to my chest. Gently I wrapped my arms around her and began rocking her as she sat on the counter saying, "Mommy's here. Mommy's here. It's OK baby."

I took Emma to her room and sat with her for a while. Then I went back to the apartment and came unglued on Ken. Furious, I said: "Logan is urinating on the walls in his room and sees lizards in his room and on his bed. Now he has attacked Emma. It is time to place him." Defiantly I glared at him, just daring him to challenge me.

At that point, Logan ran into Ken's office and grabbed the cords from his laptop computer and said he was going to choke Ken to death. Then he wrapped them around his own neck and began to choke himself. Then Logan started to hit his own arm saying he was going to break it. Next he turned on Ken and began to punch, slap and bite him. Owen was present, and an overwhelming feeling of doom came over the entire house. The tone was always dark when Owen was around, and Logan was very compliant to Owen's controlling demands. Ken took hold of Logan's head so I could place a pill in his mouth in order to calm him; he finally fell asleep watching a movie.

To everyone involved, it was apparent that the level of care Logan needed could not be provided in our house. Ken found it especially difficult to apprehend the fact that we had to hand Logan over to a facility. We grieved that the things we wanted for Logan were gone, and grieved the loss of our child. How can you pick one child over the other? Emma had a chance at a normal life and Logan did not. Emma deserved to be in a safe home and Logan was dangerous. It still felt wrong to put him away, but we had no choice.

That evening, Evelyn, Forrest and Maureen came over. Ken told them what had happened and that he agreed to place Logan in a facility. Immediately Evelyn began making calls. At one point I heard her say: "You will open a bed for him now or I will call in every favor and make sure you never work in the industry again." I remember thinking, "She may speak with southern gentility but she will rip out your jugular if you don't do what she asks." Evelyn was flawless in her execution of demands and played it so well. It was amazing to watch how she handled difficult situations without getting ruffled.

Ken started getting emotional and his voice cracked as he said, "We can't do this to Logan."

Evelyn asked, "Is that what you think? It's cute, but is also very naïve."

"I feel sorry for Logan and I don't want to send him away." Ken said.

Then Evelyn said, "We are way past feelings, Ken. Go away, you're breaking my heart."

That night, Aunt Evelyn called in every favor she had ever racked up to get Logan immediately placed in the best residential home available. Then she chartered a jet to fly him and a special medical team to his "new home" in Colorado.

The guilt I felt was horrible. I knew that deep down Ken blamed me for Logan having to leave and felt it was because I was not a good enough mother for him. Ken was never able to get past this.

Ken was very sensitive about Logan and would not discuss him with anyone. When asked, he said that Logan had gone off to a boarding school. Not one word of Logan's mental illness ever came out of Ken's mouth.

Unlike Ken, I told the truth. Why lie when the truth would do? I just asked people not to discuss Logan in front of Emma because it was too painful and fresh for her to handle. Plus, I felt guilty for being relieved that Logan was no longer with us. It was something I was deeply ashamed of and could tell no one but the counselor I saw after Logan left.

The counselor told me that it was normal to feel relief after living in a traumatic situation for seven years, and then explained that she was treating me the same way she did a battered spouse. She said that I had a version of Post-Traumatic Stress Disorder from dealing with Logan's behavior, which was why I became so anxious around crying children. She encouraged me to get a prescription of Xanax from my primary care physician and take half a pill when the anxious feelings began.

I wondered why in the world they didn't offer this to me sooner. I felt as if I was in the Vietnam War zone with Logan, always on high alert, and it was hard to break those habits. I explained to the counselor that I still ate standing up, used the bathroom as fast as possible and ran out to wash my hands in the kitchen so I could see what Logan was doing, even though he was not there. So the counselor and I started calling it in "the Nam." When I began to panic hearing children whine or cry I would go in "the Nam."

The counselor taught me how to control the feelings that come from caring for an explosive child who beat on me. I had become very good at pretending and hiding the fact that I felt anxious. I had to hide it from Logan to keep him from getting amped up by my reaction. Now I had to actually "feel my feelings" instead of hiding them.

The sad thing was I still felt guilty about Logan being taken away. I chose Emma, my own flesh and blood. Maybe I was just like Aunt Evelyn deep down. Aunt "Evil" always said that blood is thicker than water and she made it abundantly clear that people related by blood have stronger obligations to each other than to people outside of the family. I loved Logan the same as Emma even though he was not my blood. Nevertheless, I am deeply protective of Emma and want to spend the rest of my life making up for the "lost years" that were not her fault.

I hated what we did, putting Logan away. How do I recover from losing him? I am done with saying I'm sorry. Ken and I had to do it and I don't need anyone's approval to be happy. I am going to stay positive and something new and better will happen for this family. I don't want to get involved in battles that I don't need to fight. Furthermore, I am not trying to convince people that I am ok, I am just breathing in and out.

I had thrown myself into raising Logan and now it was Emma's turn once again. The counselor promised that the guilt associated with losing Logan would lesson over time and that placing my focus on Emma would help. She also pushed me to go to yoga to help me relax.

Now I have to stop asking why this happened, and why was Logan brought into our lives just to be taken away. Instead I must ask what is next. I even nurtured some hope that it would help my marriage to Ken.

To continue my healing, I decided to take up yoga. I still remember the first day I entered that hot yoga room. I placed my mat on the floor and lay down to let the heat warm my muscles. Then I breathed deeply and shook off the day, letting the tension drip off me. Next I released the negative emotions and let them fall to the ground in great drops of sweat.

Sometimes letting go is what is best, not only for my heart but for my state of mind. Finally I thought I could see a light at the end of this long, dark tunnel.

Chapter 17

Our friend, Mark, was a recovering alcoholic. Though he had been sober for a year he still attended a men's AA meeting near his and Maggie's house. During that time, he agreed to sponsor another man, Louis, who was about twenty-five-years-old. In accordance with AA practice, Mark began walking Louis through the Twelve Step program.

One night, Maggie awakened Mark at 2:00 a.m. and told him that his phone was vibrating. When he answered, she could hear a voice on the other end say, "I'm the manager of O'Henry's Bar on Haywood Street. Your buddy, Louis, is very drunk. He said I could call you and that you would come and get him."

Mark told the manager he would be right there and then asked for the address. "You can't miss it. The door has a big sign on it that says Men's Night Out" the manager said.

When Maggie asked what was going on, Mark told her that he had to go O'Henry's Bar and get Louis because he was drunk. "Isn't that a gay bar?" Maggie asked. "I believe it is" said Mark. Maggie asked if he knew that Louis was gay. Mark said, "Yes, I did. I am his sponsor and that information is private."

Mark got dressed and drove to the bar to get Louis. All the way there, he thought about how disappointed he was that he had relapsed. Nevertheless, he knew that he could not judge Louis, but had to help him over this bump in his recovery.

The first thing Mark saw when he walked into the bar was a sizable number of men in groups of two or three. Scanning the room, he finally spotted Louis slumped over at the bar. Mark shook him awake and then helped him to his feet so they could walk to the car. Louis was dragging his feet so it was difficult for Mark to hold him upright.

On the way out, Mark happened to glance over his shoulder and saw Ken sitting in a booth with another man. Immediately, Mark became very uncomfortable, so he glanced back over his shoulder again to make sure that it really was Ken. Mark's first thought was, "What is he doing here at two o'clock in the morning?" Then Ken looked him right in the eye and quickly turned away.

Mark drove Louis home and helped him inside to his couch. Then he wrote a note to Louis saying that he would pick him up for the AA meeting and then after the meeting would help him get his car.

It was almost 3:30 a.m. when Mark finally crawled back into bed with Maggie. Though he was tired, he was unable to sleep because of what he had seen at the bar. What should he do about seeing Ken? Why was he even there? Does Kate know what's going on? That morning Mark discussed it with Maggie and they agreed that he had to talk to Ken.

While driving over to get Louis, Mark called Ken. When he answered Mark asked, "Hey. What were you doing in a gay bar last night?"

"What are you talking about? I'm in Atlanta at a conference" Ken said.

"You looked right at me!" said Mark getting angry.

Ken denied it saying, "It was not me and I don't know what you are talking about. If you say one more thing about it I will sue you for defamation of character and it will get real ugly real fast!"

After an uncomfortable silence Mark said, "Are you friggin' kidding me, Ken? You know that I saw you at O'Henry's last night!" Mark was getting more and more riled up.

Ken cussed Mark out and then disconnected the call. Mark was furious so he mashed on the button to roll the window down and flung his cell phone out onto the highway. Mark knew Ken was lying!

Meanwhile, Vera was helping me and we were using the laptop in Ken's home office to research menopause for mom's hot flashes. When she entered "menopause" in the search box the drop-down history displayed "Men for Men." She gasped and then quickly yelled, "Oh, Kate."

The Shattered Faberge Egg

When I saw what Vera had found I felt the color drain from my face. "Vera, most men have no interest in gay porn sites. I am hiring a private investigator...don't say one word to Ken."

Vera knew of a local PI named John Jacobs, so I called him to ask some questions. I explained that I wanted to know if my husband was cheating or just looking at gay porn.

The PI wanted a retainer, which I agreed to pay, and then he instructed me to hire, Eric, a computer expert to examine the hard drive on Ken's laptop to see what sites he had visited. Ken had been clearing the history every day, but the PI explained the hard drive would still have all of that information recorded on it. I called the computer expert to set an appointment and then agreed to drive over to his office right away with the laptop in order to get the information quicker.

Nervously I waited while Eric looked at the hard drive. He found thirty websites Ken had visited including barebacksex.com and babylonboys.com, and had searched many times using "gay erotic stories" and "gay male massage." Eric suggested that I call our cellular phone provider to get a copy of his cell phone records and look for frequently called numbers.

This whole scene was beginning to overwhelm me. "So much for living happily ever after" I thought. Then I asked Eric what babylonboys.com was. When he pulled up the site I could see that it was gay porn featuring male models and live webcams used to stream video sex to men with memberships.

I was both infuriated and afraid of what I had discovered. Then I began to wonder what kind of hedonistic lifestyle Ken was living. He wasn't in Atlanta. The pricey PI had located him right in Asheville. He was at a hotel and had been the whole time. At this point, I had heard enough so I picked up the phone and called Ken.

"Hello. How is your day going?" Ken said.

Trying to keep my voice calm I asked, "How is the conference in Atlanta?"

"It's the same old boring stuff as always" He said.

At this point I came unglued. "I know you are a lying dog and are right here in Asheville!"

Ken became very agitated and said: "I am in Atlanta, not in Asheville. Mark is a liar and this is totally jacked up. I already told Mark that was not me. I know he thinks he saw me in a bar, but he is mistaken."

I told him that I had not talked to Mark or Maggie. Dead silence. Then Ken hung up on me. Immediately I called Maggie. Ken jumped in the Mercedes drove to Atlanta to cover his tracks. He spent a lot of time there for business.

"Maggie spill" I demanded.

Maggie told me everything that had happened. She said that Mark wanted to talk to Ken first so she promised to wait until he had. She said that she wanted to tell me but had to wait until she could figure out how. "Kate, I am so sorry. Please try to understand why I did not call you right away."

When I walked into the house Vera could see that I was furious. My hands were shaking so badly I couldn't even dial the phone, so I asked her to make a doctor appointment for me. When she asked why, I said, "I want to get tested for STDs." Vera still worked for us we did not have the heart to let her go after Logan left even though we really did not need her services. She was like family now.

After Vera called the doctor's office, I told her that I was getting rid of my collection of Staffordshire Spaniel figurines. I wanted all of those dogs out of my house. Some of the figurines were from the 19th century and were made in England and Scotland. I loved the ones that favored the King Charles Cavalier Spaniels. I began grabbing those figurines and smashing each set into the fireplace. I was flinging one after another. "Ken is out getting it on doggie style and I am not getting any. We collected these figurines all over the world just like he is collecting men doggie style."

I walked in every room the dog statues were everywhere. The rage in me helped me with smashing them in the bedroom fireplace and counting the thousands of dollars out loud as I smashed them. $1,000, $2000 threw in some more. $5,000 kept crashing them. I really let loose. "What a .... !" I screamed.

Why did we have so many of these dogs all over the house? I can't look these dogs anymore I said in a fury. I felt like Ken had stabbed me with a knife and twisted it. "$7,000 this pair was from Monte Carlo." There was a giant crash. Vera flinched every time I threw a set in the fireplace. Ceramic shards where flying everywhere. "I want to blow up this house and everything in it."

Vera asked, "Are you sure you want to keep busting them because some of the figurines were very expensive. Remember Ken was very mad when Logan broke one last year."

"Ken will really spit fire when he discovers I smashed to smithereens $15,000 in collectibles."

Vera said, "He has done some horrible things and kind of deserves some payback."

I said, "Ken was with me when I bought every one of these sets. We are scheduled to show off our collection next month at the Staffordshire Figure Association meeting. Now that I know he was acting like a dirty dog and I want to rid the house of every one of them."

The bag Vera was using to clean up the pieces was getting heavy so Vera went to get another one. I wanted to remove every dog from the house and throw them in the garbage toter in the garage. Immediately I can't stand looking at them how dare he do this to me!"

I told her, "Every vacation, every trip we went on Ken and I shopped for sets of Staffordshire dogs. I was building a collection and Ken was collecting men," I was shaking with adrenaline I was completely outraged. "These were his little trophies of his escapades for every lover he had."

"To bad Logan is not here he would have enjoyed smashing these, I miss the little booger." Vera said.

I began to cry and in spite of my anger, "I am missing my little boy so much and I keep finding his toys."

I have to get out of this house too many things to deal with… I was grieving Logan and now Ken had knocked the wind out of me. Emma and I had to get away. I just could not be here when Ken arrived.

Then I asked Vera to pack a bag for Emma because she and I were leaving town right away before I became unhinged. I just had to get out of this house.

Still seething, I put the bags into the car and drove to Atlanta with Emma. Once there, we checked into the Ritz Carlton to escape. I had to start dealing with the fact that Ken had broken my trust and it was irreparable.

This was Emma's first trip to the Ritz, but not mine. My favorite part was when the valet said, "Have you stayed with us before?" I answered, "Yes." And the valet said, "Welcome Back."

As we walked through the lobby, I told Emma that "When God takes a day off from Heaven he comes to the Ritz." She smiled as she took in the large fresh flower arrangements and chandeliers in the lobby of the hotel. I asked for a large suite and charged it on my American Express card. Then I told Emma that she had arrived in the Motherland.

While we were lying on the plush hotel bed she began to ask me questions about the Ritz. I told her about the level of service and how I admired the dark wood floors in the room. Emma was happy to hang out so we ordered room service and looked over the in-room movie choices. She chose a movie about penguins called "Happy Feet." When our luggage was delivered, the baggage attendant told Emma that the sheets were 3500 thread-count. She ran her hand over them and comment about how soft they were. He said it was because of the thread-count.

Following Ken to Atlanta the PI, John, waited for Ken to leave his hotel. He noted in his log that Ken Burnett left the building and drove to a parking lot. John parked as well and followed Ken as he walked down the street for about ten minutes before darting into a Men's only club. He walked right in past the front desk without stopping, giving the attendant a nod as he went by.

John stopped at the desk and was told that he needed to be a member to enter, so he filled out the paperwork and paid the fee. Once inside he was handed a towel and a locker key. John saw other men disrobing and wrapping the towels around their mid-section. He walked down the corridor and saw more men either completely nude or standing with towels wrapped around their waists. The club was large with rooms lining the hallway each with the door open. He saw that there was a gym, showers, sauna and Jacuzzi as well. TV's lined the walls playing gay porn and there were social lounges for the men and endless mirrors. Every room had bowls filled with condoms and lubricant.

One man John spotted wore a wedding ring. As he passed by a room he saw a man kneeling in front of another man while several other men watched. When the act was over, the man picked up his towel and left. No one spoke, but using their eyes and holding a glance a little long they made silent agreements to participate in sex. Music was playing in the background and John noticed a framed poster on the wall promoting safe sex.

Still looking for Ken, John continued searching as he passed the sauna room and a large hot tub that could hold up to twenty men. Then he spotted Ken entering a room so he followed him to see what would happen next. Ken went into the social lounge, laid on the bed and waited. The PI John went to sit in the couch area in the corner of the same room feeling completely uncomfortable in his towel and was ready to leave. Some men in the lounge had multiple partners with no strings attached and others only wanted to be with one partner.

Not wanting to stare, John looked around the room and noticed a wall of "glory holes" and members standing behind the wall watching and waiting.

Afterwards Ken stood up picking up his towel and went to shower off. Then he walked into the hot tub and pool area. Ken stopped and spoke with some men he seemed to know by the pool.

After the group of men were finished talking, Ken went back to his locker and began to get dressed. It was apparent Ken spent time here often. John waited a few minutes to exit and then raced out to see if Ken's car was still in the parking lot. It was, and Ken was on the phone still in the parking space. Quickly, John snuck to his car and followed as Ken drove back to his hotel.

John had seen lots of things in his career, but this left him feeling dirty. Shaking it off, he began to prepare a report.

I was way ahead of him and ready for information when I went into the bathroom turned on the shower so Emma could not hear me talking and sat on the edge of the marble tub. Dialing the phone, I could feel the plush white Ritz Carlton robe against my skin. Emma was asleep and the bathroom door was closed. As I looked around the posh interior, I could see my reflection in the polished white marble floor.

"Hello, Mrs. Burnett" John said.

"Please. Call me Kate. What did Ken do today?" I asked. "Where did he go?"

"You may want to sit down Kate….."

Barely able to breathe, I dialed the phone again. "The report I just got from the private investigator about Ken reads like a demon's resume. I had no idea how involved he was in the gay lifestyle. Ken is totally immersed."

Hearing my sister's voice caused my resolve to crumble. I slumped down onto that cold marble floor and sobbed. I was shattered. I had just lost my beautiful little boy and now Ken had betrayed me. The words tumbled from my mouth as I poured out my heart to Jill. I could barely speak from crying as I told her the details of what I had just learned. Thank God the shower was still on and the door was locked. I could never allow Emma to see me this way. For Emma, I would be strong.

"We are on the way to the Ritz and will be there in a few hours" Jill said. "Just hold it together for Emma." Then I heard her say, "Momma. You and I are going to Atlanta to be with Kate and Emma. She just found out that Ken is gay and has been cheating on her with men, so we're driving down to the Ritz. Emma will stay with you so you can entertain her while I help Kate sort this out."

My mother put her face in her hands and began to cry. "First Logan and now this?" she thought.

Chapter 18

Our mom Suzanne and Emma stayed in one room at the Ritz so Jill and I could be alone in another room for long discussions about what to do next. The first thing I wanted to do was drive by the Men only clubs that were in Atlanta. There were four main clubs. Some were converted warehouses and others were bath houses. The club that Ken had been followed to by the PI had a plain looking front door that was tinted so that you could not see inside and there was a sign on the front of the door that said Men's Only Private club. I told Jill I just could not believe that this is where Ken goes when he is supposed to be working. I felt numb and Jill told me to stop pretending like things were ok.

John, the private investigator I hired, continued to follow Ken and record his random hook-ups. When he called me with his latest findings, I couldn't believe what I was hearing.

1. Ken went to Fantasy Festival in Ft. Lauderdale with David Talent. David was a single man who was a long-term friend of ours and lived in our neighborhood. I had always suspected he was gay.

2. The P.I. discovered that David was Ken's steady boyfriend but Ken continued to engage in random sex with other men. He was cheating on both his boyfriend and his wife. He was like an addict who loved the cheating and sneaking as much as the sex. He enjoyed the danger of being caught, but "Captain Entitlement" was so narcissistic he believed he would never be exposed. He engaged in risky behavior just for the thrill of it.

3. Ken took me to lunch at the club and then met our waiter for a sexual encounter that afternoon.

It was hard to hear these things about my husband. At first shame washed over me, and then I became furious. I could not believe that Ken was doing those things. John said, "Kate, I am sorry you are going through this." I thanked him and said that I would rather know the truth so I could deal with it.

When Ken came home 2 days later, he acted like everything was normal. He quickly said hello, kissed Emma and immediately went to take a shower. Still reeling from everything John reported, I was repulsed at seeing him yet desperate for confirmation from his "boyfriend." Without hesitation, I took his cell phone and dialed David Talent's number. When David answered, I quickly hung up and then, with heart pounding, decided to redial the number. The phone rang and David answered saying, "Ken, are you there?" Breathless, I hung-up again.

I was incensed, but wanting to confront Ken I walked into the master bathroom with his phone in my hand. "How long have you been sleeping with David Talent?" I asked. Without skipping a beat Ken answered, "Why don't you just tell everybody you found out my big secret?" Taken by surprise with his answer, all I could do was lay his phone on the bathroom counter and leave the room.

In the kitchen my mind was racing when Ken walked in and said, "I have no idea what you are talking about. I suppose that from now on you'll think that I'm sleeping with every man I talk to. David is just a friend from high school and that's all. You really need to chill out or else I will tell everyone that you have had affairs our whole marriage."

"You lied to me! The bonds of our marriage are broken! You cheated and lied! Who cares if you cheated with a man or woman? You are living a secret life.

"I expected you to stop dating when we got married. I am angry...you have cheated during our whole marriage. I know because I checked the hard drives on every computer, even the old desktop, from when we were first married. I know everything." I said.

"Look. You were on the rebound from losing the love of your life and I was the perfect Band-Aid to your situation. It's not like I was your soul mate or anything." Ken said.

"You don't deserve me!" I cried. "I loved you as my husband and as the father of our children. You only tolerated me to appear straight, and you made me doubt myself as a woman. I did everything possible to make myself look good for you, but you lied to yourself more than you lied to me. Pretending to be someone you are not is no way to live. How do you sleep at night? You lay in bed beside me and were cheating on me the entire marriage. I feel so humiliated!"

When I told Ken that I wanted a divorce, he yelled back at me and said, "We are staying married! We will not get a divorce!" Then he threatened me: "I will take Emma away from you and tell everyone that you are a pill junkie and a drunk. I will prove that you are an unfit mother and my family will pay-off every judge in the county so it will stick." He was so sure that he would win.

Cold fear began to rise up within me as I realized how deviant Ken really was. For him it was all about winning. He cared more about looking good in front of others than he did about dragging Emma and me through hell.

I backed down and said, "Emma is the most important thing in my life and I only want what is best for her. You are controlling and difficult, but no matter what kind of a lying monster you are you will always be Emma's father, so I will never take her away from you. You're a good father but a terrible husband." This was the first time I was actually scared of Ken and his money, but I had had enough and was not going to let him off the hook this time.

Ken needed to understand that I knew everything about his gay antics: massages by gay men that included whatever you would want. Rentboy.com and Craig's list adventures I knew it all. I explained to him about the private investigator and that I had evidence of everything he had been doing.

I told Ken that I knew that Aunt Evil (Evie) had sent him to a counselor for reparative therapy to cure him of homosexuality. When that didn't work she contacted Exodus International to help him with conversion therapy. I believed he could not change because he had practiced this so long it had become a stronghold in his life and I told him so. I struggled because I loved the man I thought Ken was, but not who he actually was. It was hard to deal with the fact that every memory I had about our marriage was nothing more than lies.

Ken had treated me like his slave, and that made me very angry. I had been his faithful wife for a decade. Who admits to having lovers their entire marriage? Then I started remembering things that had happened and bells went off. Finally it started making sense. On our trip to France, Ken booked massages with male and female massage therapists. He asked me which one I wanted, and me, being compliant as always, said that it didn't matter so Ken chose the man. The very next night Ken said he was going out shopping and left me alone for a couple of hours to watch a movie. Jill was upset when she found out because she felt we should have shared a romantic dinner not leave me to have room service. This was when Travis first began to suspect that Ken was a practicing homosexual.

I remembered a conversation with Ken about why we never had sex. He gave me the lame excuse that after seeing Emma being born he had lost interest. I was surprised because I thought men wanted to have sex with beautiful women all the time.

Finally I told Ken: "I have complied with everything you have ever wanted of me. Was there ever a time when you felt love for me?" He just sat there silent so I asked, "How do you feel about me?" He said, "Indifferent."

When I asked Ken why he married me he said, "You still had faith in people. You were so naïve you believed that people were basically good. You were heartbroken and on the rebound. It was easy to sweep you off your feet. You bought the whole thing hook, line, and sinker. You were conned. Deal with it, Kate. Grow up! It was almost too easy...storybook easy. So it happened. Get over it. You're not leaving me and I'm not admitting to anyone that I'm gay. I will never give you a divorce and I will never move out of this house. You will stay here for Emma and act like nothing is different."

When I shook my head "No," Ken's response was, "What are you going to do about it? How's that positive thinking working for you now?"

The Shattered Faberge Egg

"Look at the deception constantly mocking me" I said. "You will be paid back for all the evil you have done. You have utterly rejected me for the last time. Your heart is empty."

"Why don't you just go back to the trailer where I found you and be the white trash you are?" Ken smirked. I knew he was having fun prodding me into a rage, I still could not believe the things he was saying just to get a rise out of me. Calling me white trash just to be mean was just cruel. "I married the fantasy life you promised me, Ken, but I also expected you to love me."

Ken said that he was not capable of loving me, so I told him that I would not stay married to him. From that moment I began to insulate my heart from further hurt. I told him, "If you want to have sex with men then do it. Just let me go. Leave me out of it."

Ken proceeded to tell me that his family knew all along that he was gay. After years of secrets and lies, the pain was unbearable for me. Tears rolled down my face, but I made no sound. Instead, I got a paper towel, wiped my face, and buried my feelings deep inside as I had learned to do with Logan.

"You are such a stupid woman Kate. We all knew. My family had files and dossiers on girls to pick from and we picked you. You had no father, no brothers and you had the pedigree and polish we needed in a wife. I needed to get married to protect the family image. My whole family knows I am gay.

"You were used by more than one person. I wanted children and needed a wife to cover my secret. Kate, this is the real world. Now you are going to shut-up and deal with it. We are going to stay married for Emma's sake and you are going to keep silent. You will never divorce me. No one would walk away from money like this. And if you do try and divorce me, you are in for the fight of your life. My family will take my side and unite against you to take Emma."

My blood began to boil. Old repressed deep-seated anger rose in me and I exploded!

Looking Ken straight in the eyes and with every ounce of resolve I could muster, I told him, "I want a divorce you lying dog. You worked me like a slave watching the kids and keeping up with this house, holding a job, and entertaining friends. I have been a loyal, faithful and good wife. You treated me like scum. You could have exposed me to all kinds of diseases…"

To which Ken said, "No they always used a condom." I wanted to smack him!

I said, "Oh, you were the one receiving. That's just perfect."

"Kate I am gay, I like men."

"But you are married to me" I said.

"You had better brace yourself because you are in for the fight of your life" Ken replied.

"I can't believe you were having affair or one night stands and casual sex during our marriage. Other days you acted like my best friend. You were my best friend." I said.

"Kate, I feel sorry for you."

"How long did you go without a lover during our marriage?"

"Three months." Ken said.

"Ken, you always treated me as a possession behind closed doors, but in front of others you treated me like royalty. That is why I always wanted to entertain. I have a perfectly good reason to divorce you and get out. You were hard to live with before I found out you were gay. Now it will be impossible. You didn't want a wife you wanted an incubator, a nanny and a maid, a baby maker and cook. Why didn't you hire a surrogate?"

"Things were different" Ken said. "You couldn't just be gay and out. I was gay before it was acceptable. Asheville was not as open then as San Francisco."

My head was spinning. Past thoughts, events and memories were flooding in and bells were going off as I remembered the way things had been:

- ✓ Ken never looked at other women
- ✓ He was never jealous of men flirting with me
- ✓ He was always concerned with his hair and clothes

- ✓ Gay-porn on the computer screen that he said was a pop up, but got angry when I walked in on him
- ✓ Always took a shower right when he came home
- ✓ He never touched me

Everything was starting to make sense. I felt like such a fool as these thoughts flooded my mind.

Years of lingerie, tan lines, perfume, new haircuts, new panties, and coming on to Ken. I remembered all the things I did to try to get his attention. I was relieved to figure out he was batting for the other side and he liked to catch. There was nothing I could have ever done to tantalize Captain Entitlement.

Now I wanted freedom. Freedom from this ridiculous prison camp Ken had trapped me in. Poor Emma! She lost a brother and her mother and father were fighting. Ken was vindictive and wanted retaliation, so I had no idea what was coming next. I didn't care anymore…he had gone too far.

One day while out shopping, I saw a doormat that said, "Back door guests are best." I laughed to myself, bought it, and put it by the garage door knowing it would make Ken mad.

T.T. Johnson

Chapter 19

As the days and weeks wore on, my resolve strengthened but I was still heartbroken. I had been so caught-up in the glitz and glamour of the Burnett family and the way they had seemed to accept me that I was blind to what was really going on. Looking back I can see many things Ken did that should have been a red flag. He refused to wear his wedding ring to the pool or the beach because he said he did not want a tan line from it. I feel so stupid now for not realizing he took his ring off so he could cheat without that being an indication he was married. I was completely blind to it all and not looking for it because I trusted him. As it turned out, Ken had been juggling men like he would a hobby. His behavior had contaminated our marriage and broken it.

When Ken received notice that I had filed for divorce he was furious. That night when he came in from work he asked if I needed to tell him something. Then he said, "I got a receipt in the mail for a retainer for a lawyer you hired. You know that I don't like surprises, so get that money back right now! Do you understand me?"

"What did you expect me to do once I found out, Ken? I have done everything you have ever asked me to do and I have been a faithful wife. What hurts the most is that I have given my best through the good times and the bad times, and have been the glue that has held our relationship together. Through it all I stuck by you but you continued to pull away. You stopped fighting <u>for</u> me and just fought with me. You don't try at all anymore. We can't buy happiness. We are either happy or we are not. It's obvious that you are not happy in this marriage and never will be."

"Yes, you caught me, but you will never walk away from the money so I'm not worried at all." Ken said. Then he left the room laughing, really believing that I would not leave.

Later that evening I was kissing Emma good night when she asked, "Why are you and daddy getting a divorce? Is it because daddy loves someone else?"

I said, "Emma, your daddy and I love you very much. This is not mommy's fault and it is not your fault. Someday when you are older I will explain it to you." Thankfully she didn't ask any more questions, so I stayed with her until she fell asleep.

After Emma fell asleep, I went downstairs and called my mom in Charleston. "I have lots of guilt for not seeing this and it is humiliating me. I never thought Ken could be so vindictive. The only thing I did was discover his secret life." Mom said that he conned her too and said I should try not to feel bad. Just talking to her and learning that he had fooled her as well helped take some of the sting away.

To get back at me, Ken began telling anyone who would listen that I was having affairs, which was the real reason our marriage was on the rocks. He said that I had slept with our nanny, Vera, and a man at work.

When I found out what Ken was spreading as gossip, I became so angry I could hardly see straight. Immediately I called him and confronted him. "How dare you say I had affairs? While you were giving out passes to your ass, I was consumed with taking care of Logan. If I must, I will take a polygraph test to prove that I have been faithful to you for our entire marriage" Like I had time or energy to cheat while being beaten by Logan. Again, he hung up on me.

Next I phoned Vera and told her about the lies Ken was spreading. "No offense," I said, "but I am not attracted to tall women." Vera laughed and said, "None taken, I would never do you but I know you want my ghetto fantastic wigs." I laughed out loud and then Vera said, "He is the queen of 'tail-gating.'" It felt good to have someone who was on my side and could laugh with me about the whole mess. Vera was more than an employee she was a friend.

Jill and Travis found a certified licensed polygraph examiner and made an appointment for me to take a polygraph exam. When I arrived at the office I was greeted by Mr. McCallister, a professional looking man with white hair who took me into the testing room. Mr. McCallister said, "Sexual relations are understood to include any oral, anal and vaginal contact." I gulped and wondered what I had gotten myself into, but signed the consent forms anyway.

Mr. McCallister told me that the video camera was on and then he placed leads at various points on my body. He explained that he would ask questions while measuring my breathing, pulse and galvanic skin responses. He began by asking…

Since your marriage to Ken Burnett have you had sexual relations with anyone else?

Did you ever have sex with a boss or co-worker?

Did you ever have sexual relations with Vera your nanny?

I answered "No" to all the questions.

After asking me the last question, Mr. McCallister left the room to compile his report. After about thirty minutes he returned and went over the results with me. His last statement was the one upon which I staked my claim: "Mrs. Burnett, the evidence indicates truthful test results."

Smiling, I left with the report and began planning how, when and to whom I should send the "Detection of Deception" exam results. I made copies of the eight-page report that included Mr. McCallister's résumé of specialized training and mailed one to Aunt Evil, Forrest and Meanie, and Robert, Ken's brother.

For once I had hard evidence in my hand that validated my feelings. Ken had abused me enough and I would not let him continue to spread lies about me after cheating on me for years. He was an insecure bully and I was done being manipulated by him, a spoiled brat who felt entitled to whatever he wanted, and an arrogant backstabber who was so cold that he lied when the truth would have been easier to tell.

I was surprised to learn that Robert actually opened the letter and read the polygraph report. He told me that he knew Ken was lying about all the things I had supposedly done.

It was no surprise that Aunt Evelyn refused her copy by writing, "Return to Sender" on the envelope in her own handwriting. When I saw it returned in the mailbox, I knew that she had read every word, probably Forrest's copy, and refused her letter just to get at me. They all knew that Ken was gay, but wanted nobody else to know.

A week or two later, I went out on the front porch one afternoon to read. Lee Yung, a young man I knew who managed the grocery store, drove by and stopped when he saw me. He was about twenty-five-years-old, gay, and in college.

"Ms. Kate, I want to tell you that it is not your fault and you did nothing wrong." Lee said that he knew Ken was gay the first time he met us. When I asked how he knew, Lee told me that it was the way Ken looked in his eyes and his mannerisms. He went on to tell me how things were different these days and that a guy he knows from his fraternity just got married and has an open marriage with his wife. They each have sex with other people at parties. He said that group sex was more the norm these days and that it was no big deal.

The more Lee told me, the more I felt as if I had been sequestered away somewhere. However, what he said was very interesting. I was beginning to think I had no idea what people were doing sexually. I knew that I had been in a holding pattern for seven years watching Logan's every move, but this was too much.

"So 'three-ways' are normal now?" I asked Lee. He just looked at me with pity in his eyes. I realized then that I was a sexual infant and that Ken had liked it that way. All through our marriage, he would never experiment with me sexually. I felt very naïve. But, gay sex? Group sex? Others watching?

My thoughts turned to how difficult dating must have become. In a world where porn is so accessible how could I compete and make it.

"Lee," I said, "When I was in college there were only couples. And I did not even know what a ménage-a-trios' was. I thought to myself how Ken wanted to wait to have sex until we got married. I thought it was because Ken had strong morals not because he did not like women.

Lee laughed and said, "I really just wanted to say you did nothing wrong, and that it is not your fault. You are a beautiful woman Ms. Kate. By the way, are you aware of the high population of gay men that live in this neighborhood?" I felt really duped

After talking to Lee I felt concerned at what Emma would be facing one day when she began dating What were they thinking? I chuckled to myself. The people at that church had furious intensity and spread the gossip about Ken and the gossip storm raged for months.

Later that week, the Burnett's called a family meeting to discuss the "situation." I wasn't involved, but learned everything that happened from Robert. He surprised me by telling me how bad he felt for me and wondered how I was going to handle everything. Then he shared how he thoroughly enjoyed watching his brother being raked over the coals.

Robert told me that Aunt Evie was the first to confront Ken. "You are coming out of the closet even if I have to drag you out." Robert quipped, "Would that make him a 'drag queen'?" Evie did not think that was funny and told Robert to shut-up. She was running for Congress and wanted to use Ken's "coming out" as a campaign issue. She felt the time was ripe for gay rights to take center stage and thought it would be excellent in her platform. Then she said, "This is your fault Ken, you got careless and went to a gay bar in Asheville. We can't contain this any longer." Robert said, "You were supposed to be getting your wedgie on in Atlanta not locally."

Ken's mother jumped to his defense and said, "Ken can't come out now. What about Emma?"

With a look that would wilt an oak tree, Aunt Evil hissed at Maureen, "It's too late! Your narcissist son got sloppy. He was not careful. You will just have to get over it. Besides, I have my people working on how to break the story."

Robert, loving the drama before him, said. "Well, <u>Broke Back Mountain</u> is still in the theaters. Maybe that will help with the sympathy vote. Besides, Momma, you've known that he was gay since he rolled plastic Easter eggs in his t-shirt sleeves and danced around pretending to be Snow White... gives whole new meaning to dancing queen. He's hidden it for years; it's time for him to come out."

"What are we doing about Kate?" Forrest said.

"Kate who, screw Kate!" Aunt Evie said, "She is expendable and we have already had her office packed and her office locks changed, security won't be letting her back in the building. Her work cell was disconnected yesterday."

Robert couldn't keep quiet. "You know, don't you, that Ken's favorite band during high school was Duran Duran? If you didn't, his obsession with George Michael from Wham should have been another clue."

"Robert. You are not helping." said Maureen.

"Robert, speak again and you will have to ice your balls." said Evelyn.

Aunt Evelyn's cell phone rang so she shushed the whole family before answering it. While listening to the caller, she wrote down what was being said, repeating it out loud as she made a list:

- "Join PFLAG."
- "Disney's Gay day. Show support."
- "March in Washington in October."
- "Divorce Kate quietly and throw 100% support into same sex marriage and gay rights."
- "Get joint custody of Emma. Push devoted father agenda."

When the call ended, Aunt Evelyn said, "We threaten Kate with losing Emma all together and then she will sign whatever we want."

With Ken as her 'poster child,' Evelyn's campaign platform became mental health advocacy, gay rights and same sex marriage. To make it all work, Evelyn had her "damage control" team engineer Ken's life to bring the maximum benefit to her campaign. As a result, David and Ken openly lived together and accompanied Evelyn to a gay rights march that October in Washington DC. With her platform being what it was, they could explain losing Logan, Ken being gay, and he and David living together. In Evelyn's words, "We use it all for the campaign."

Ken had always flaunted his wealth and bought things to make up for his lack of self-esteem that came from living a secret life. He lived a lie instead of being who he really was, but now he was forced to come out and be open. Only time would tell as to whether Ken was strong enough to occupy this different niche in Asheville society. Though times were changing and attitudes along with it, the Burnett family fit in best with the more conservative elements, and now that was changing as well.

T.T. Johnson

Chapter 20

Ken's attacks on my character were taking their toll, so I was excited when Maggie called and asked if I wanted to go to dinner. At the restaurant we each ordered a glass of wine and began to talk about everything that was going on. When she told me about seeing Ken and David riding through the neighborhood on new Vespa scooters I just shook my head. I couldn't believe how they were flaunting their "coming out." Giggling, Maggie said, "I guess Ken likes the wind on his va-jay-jay." I almost spit wine across the table as we both burst out laughing.

"How could I have not known?" I asked.

"Honey, Ken had us all fooled, although the Burberry Plaid should have been a sign," Maggie replied.

"Yes. You're right. That should have been a red flag," I said. Looking back, there were so many things that should have raised a flag. "Captain Entitlement" was always hard to live with and everything was always about him. I felt like I was "Team Cheerios" and Ken was "Team Fruit Loops."

Maggie said, "Hell hath no fury like a gay man scorned!"

"You're not kidding!" I replied. "He is spending a fortune dragging me to court, deliberately making my life a living hell. Without fail, right before we walk into court, his lawyer grabs my lawyer and pans out a deal. But it still costs me $3,000 every time my attorney prepares to go before the judge."

Maggie frowned. "That's terrible Kate."

I said, "Ken knows that I cannot afford the legal fees and I'm drowning in debt trying to keep up. My mom gave me $10,000 to help with the attorney who once worked at the firm, but I can't ask her to help anymore. She lives on a fixed income since selling the practice after daddy died."

"Why is Ken being so hateful when he was the one having gay affairs and living the secret life?" Maggie asked.

"Ken is an emotionally constipated adolescent with extravagant spending habits," I replied sarcastically. "He does everything to excess. He wants me to feel the burn of outing him from my life, so he is doing anything he can to cripple me financially."

"Consider yourself lucky" Maggie said. "Ken's arms look like they belong on a T-Rex. You deserve better than a closeted gay man with lady fingers." I snickered when Maggie said that and told her that the only thing that got any action in our bedroom was the snooze button.

The red wine had warmed me and the laughter fed my soul. I sank back in the mahogany booth enjoying the moment with my dear friend. Unfortunately, all the crap I was going through kept flooding my thoughts, and then I remembered another thing that had happened. My friend, Belinda, and I were shopping when she showed me a foundation in a tube that had a brush on the end of it. She said it had great coverage and highly recommended it. I decided to buy one, but when the sales clerk ran my credit card it was declined. I was humiliated, but Belinda understood and bought it for me.

Maggie couldn't believe it and asked what happened. I told her that Ken had cancelled all of my credit cards, suspended my cell service and stopped paying the health insurance. "Travis, Jill's husband, told me that just when I thought it could not get any worse it would, and that I needed to be very careful. He warned me that I have to be prepared, and he was right."

"I am so sorry honey." Maggie said. She was such a dear friend and always on my side.

Then Maggie asked how it was going with Ken and me sharing the house. "I hate it!" I told her. "Ken stays with Emma fifteen nights a month and I stay with her the other fifteen nights. The rest of the time I stay with family and Ken stays with David. It is very stressful moving in and out, but that is the arrangement the attorneys worked out to keep Emma from being uprooted from her familiar surroundings."

"Oh, and get this. When Ken leaves he takes half of my shoes with him." Maggie couldn't believe it. I explained that Ken would not leave me a matching pair of shoes so I packed my clothes and kept suitcases in my car.

"That is insane Kate. You can't keep living like that" Maggie said.

JoAnne and Belinda finally arrived. After they sat down and ordered wine, they insisted on an instant replay of what Maggie and I had been talking about. After catching them up JoAnne said, "Kate, you have to move out, this is ridiculous." I told them that Ken had sworn that he would never move out of the house and would never pay any alimony or child support. The girls just stared at me. JoAnne said, "What father refuses to pay child support for his daughter?" Belinda piped in, "Haven't you been through enough losing Logan and then finding out Ken was gay?"

Joanne said that there was a house for rent around the corner from her and suggested that I move out. Just talking it through with my friends helped me to see that it was probably the best thing to do. Then Belinda said "Ken will never leave that house, and you can't keep living like this. One of you has to move." Maggie agreed and said, "Since Ken refuses to sell the house you should leave."

"I think you're right," I said. "My sister has to be tired of me living with her for fifteen days each month. Besides, I need my own space where I can relax."

"Ken lives at his stud muffin's house on the fifteen days he is not with Emma" JoAnne said. "That sounds like a ticket for a joyride through hell." The wine was talking now and my friends were getting bold with their advice to me. " Ken has left a trail of 100 miles of hootchie and take it like a man is what he is good at." said Belinda.

"Nobody understands how devastating and life-destroying this has been to Kate," Belinda said. "You need to move out, move on, and start doing some Internet dating." Maggie piped in with, "That's right. Your corpse of a marriage has long been cold."

"Yes," I replied, "Ken and David have been together a lot longer than people think. Even though they both have been promiscuous they function like a couple. Now that Evelyn is running for North Carolina

Congress she is pushing her same-sex marriage agenda and supporting Ken's gay lifestyle. She is also using mental illness awareness as a platform, and the Center she is building is almost completed."

"Speaking of mental illness, how is Logan doing?" Joanne asked.

"I really don't know. Ken's family won't give me an update. The last I heard he was on medication in a locked facility. Emma said that she read an email to Ken from Logan's doctor that said Logan was only aware of the present five minutes and that he did not have the ability to miss us. Logan was different emotionally, when visually stimulated he was happy, but never asked about us."

"Oh Kate, I am so sorry," Joanne said.

I cringed and then replied, "I'm dealing with the guilt of not raising Logan, and the guilt of feeling relief at not having to."

"Oh Kate, you did the best you could," Maggie said as she put her arm around my shoulder. "No one could handle him. Logan is where he needs to be."

Belinda chimed in and said, "Girls. Let's get Kate started on some Internet dating!" We really needed to cut-off Belinda's wine! JoAnne joined in and said, "Kate gets a do-over! I am all in." Belinda said, "Kate you need to get a new job and move out. I can get you a job as a loan officer at the bank where I work!"

I must confess that I never thought my motto would be "Eat; Drink; and Remarry." I wasn't sure where life was taking me, but at least it was starting to look a little more positive.

Not long after that dinner with my friends, I signed the lease on a rental house a few streets over from Ken and his "Barbie Dream House." He wasn't happy that I was moving out and he threw a fit when I asked about dividing up the furniture. He reluctantly agreed to go through the house and put a sticky note on anything that he wanted to keep and agreed to let me have what he did not want. I was just happy to be out of the house, free of everything it stood for and free of Ken at last. When I went to look at what furniture Ken chose, I nearly fell down because he wanted to keep the nine gold-framed mirrors hanging in the house. His vanity and total self- absorption was more

The Shattered Faberge Egg

than apparent to me. He thought he was the center of his own universe. He was a narcissist.

Moving day came and the attorneys agreed that Ken would not be at the house while I moved out. An hour after the movers started, Ken showed up and walked in the door. I said, "You are not allowed to be here," and then called my lawyer, who told me to videotape Ken in the house.

Shortly after that Ken's phone rang. It was his lawyer telling him to leave the house as he was in violation of our agreement. Ken got in his car and drove off, but literally twenty-minutes later, he and David came back and walked in the front door. Ken stated, "I want to be sure you are not taking anything more than you are suppose too." I called my lawyer and once again he said to videotape Ken in violation of the court agreement.

When I began videotaping Ken became very agitated and said that he would not be kicked out of his own home. I told him that I just wanted to move out in peace and that he promised not to interfere. Angrily, Ken walked over and slapped the video camera out of my hand. The blow knocked me backward and the camera hit me on the arm. Ken did not mean to hurt me he just did not want to be filmed but the blow knocked me backward and the camera hit me on the arm. My attorney wanted retribution and demanded I call 911 but the officers arrived after Ken and David had left. There was a bruise on my arm where the camera hit me so I took a photo of it.

The 911 call infuriated the Burnett's. Ken lied and told his family that the incident never happened. Despite me having it recorded Ken was a gifted liar and they chose to believe him. The queen vampire, Aunt Evil, had a conniption fit. I felt I needed a wooden stake and a silver bullet for protection. The Burnett's knew every judge in town so to pursue it would be futile. Besides, after the beatings I had endured from Logan a bruise on the arm wasn't a big deal. My attorney was very upset that I dropped it and said we could bring Ken up on criminal charges and use that against him but I was just afraid. Ken's family would pay off every judge and I would just go deeper into debt. I had no way to pay my attorney fees to date. I wanted the divorce to be settled so I could get on with my life and was tired of fighting.

The first night in my new home was lonely, but after unpacking all day I was tired. I just wanted a hot bath and to get into bed. I was unable to make myself turn off most of the lights, and I activated the alarm. The horrible feeling gnawing at me was fear. I was afraid.

Ken was happy to get rid of the old "ball and chain," but I felt like a flock of birds being sucked into a jet engine. "No amount of money is worth this," I thought. I just wanted the nightmare to be over and to be free of Ken's grasp. Until the divorce was settled, Ken was supposed to pay my car note, car insurance, cell phone and health insurance but he had already cancelled the insurance for Emma and me. He was in no hurry to settle because he wanted my lawyer fees to continue increasing. He had an endless supply of money to throw at the divorce and I had none. He had a safety net that I did not have.

The day came when I was scheduled to appear in court so I met my attorneys at their office and we all rode to the court house together. As I was getting in the back seat of the attorney's SUV, he assisted me by opening the door. I didn't like my lawyer, but was in too deep financially to bail out at this point in the process. He was an old friend of my mom's but he was milking the whole process to make money.

He was in no hurry to settle this case and just kept racking up the fees.

During the proceeding, the judge began dividing up our debts and assigning them to both Ken and me. He said that my half was $250,000 in credit card debt and half of the mortgage, $750,000. Ken was pushing for joint custody of Emma and no child support, stating that I made more money than him since he was unemployed. How convenient. I was sitting in court so upset the only thought in my head was, "I'm a million dollars in debt with no means to pay it!"

I could do nothing about it so I decided to figure out a way to reach a settlement. The next day, I made an appointment with a bankruptcy lawyer without anyone knowing about it. He was an older man and very understanding of my predicament. He explained to me that if I made less than $32,000 I could declare bankruptcy and write off my legal bills and the marital debt that I owed. I met the qualification so I began the process immediately. Now that I was going to work as a loan officer I would be earning money so the bankruptcy needed to happen before the divorce was final and my income went up.

My legal fees were gargantuan, I mean colossal in size which I had only paid $30,000, which was ridiculous since my legal counsel had accomplished nothing for me. I knew he was milking this for all he could. Meanwhile, Ken was using a criminal defense lawyer that was kicking my lawyer's butt. Aunt Evil had every judge in her back pocket, so no matter what, this divorce was never going to end well for me.

To everyone's surprise, I fired my lawyer who probably cried liked a little girl when he found out that I declared bankruptcy and then signed divorce papers agreeing that I would receive no money from Ken or the Burnett family. I agreed to joint custody of Emma since Ken had threatened to take her away from me if I did not sign the papers refusing child support. I believed he would keep me tied up in court forever, so I signed away both alimony and child support and gave him joint custody.

Though I felt as if I were signing away my life, I felt freedom like I had not known for many years. I was finally free. Free at last!

T.T. Johnson

Chapter 21

Several months after my divorce was final I was becoming very lonely, so I decided to let Belinda and JoAnne help me set up a profile on E Hamony and Match.com. Times had changed since I had graduated from college, but I wasn't sure that online match-making was for me.

To help me get started, JoAnne wrote my profile. As I read it I began to laugh and said "Is this really me? It seems so weird."

Belinda told me that "everyone" was doing it and that she knew two women who met their second husbands online. She was reading down through the list of people signed up online when she squealed and said she saw a name that we all knew. "Look! Robyn Paxtor is on here." "Wow!" I said, "she's been on more wieners than mustard." We all snickered and then Belinda said, "The best part of starting over is never looking back."

The next day I checked to see if anyone had read my profile. I saw a couple of responses that looked interesting so I set up a lunch date with one of them. I figured lunch was a safe option because I could use the excuse of having to get back to work in case he got any ideas. On the other hand, if I liked him I could set up drinks or dinner for another time. I quickly discovered however, that these men were only interested in one thing. I decided the whole thing should be called "I buy you dinner and we have sex.com" or "Wham, Bam, Scam Dating."

During one lunch date, right in the middle of the conversation, my "date" said, "Kate, I do very well when I am on my medication." I asked him what condition he took medication for and he said, "Bipolar Disorder." I blocked his calls right after lunch.

Despite the obvious weirdos, I didn't give up and spent many months dating and acclimating myself to that whole scene. I had conversations by phone or email and kept the details of each man in the dating cesspool clear by using a notebook. Some of the men I encountered included:

- ✓ One guy with a facial twitch you could see from space.
- ✓ A man I named "Hunka Hunka Burning Love" because he had Elvis hair and mutton chops. I quickly left the building.
- ✓ Another date was very attractive and ordered me a glass of wine. Then he said, "I am uncircumcised, is that a problem?" I said, "No, but talking about your ding-a-ling before dinner is." I excused myself and walked out. (Maggie howled with laughter when I reported in on this date and said, "Kate, You are weeding them out for sure.")
- ✓ The straw that broke the Internet camel's back was the serial dater who ambush kissed me before dinner at the hostess stand.

I told the girls that none of the men looked like their pictures. I named one guy "Liar, Liar Pants on Fire" because he was super short and had a large space in his front teeth, none of which was revealed in his photos. When I told him I needed to go to the restroom, I excused myself and just kept walking right out to my car and went home.

Maggie suggested I try using a Christian website, so I did. That was when I discovered that many of those guys are not so Christian. Casual sex was rampant among them as well, which seems to be how dating is nowadays. The guys want to open the condom before the dinner check arrives. I wanted to find a husband not have a fling. I wanted a long term commitment.

I told Maggie about one guy that had so much back hair sprouting out of his shirt that he could have used it as a toupee. It was awful. When she asked what I had called him I said, "Pack of hot dogs, because the back of his neck looked like a pack of hot dogs." By that point I had decided to go back to meeting dates at Starbuck's so that I didn't waste my time. Some dates started out okay, but then I would discover they had three kids, or no job, or they smelled like incense. I had only met two guys that seemed normal that I continued to see. I kept trying to get to know them better, but it seemed useless.

Maggie said that it didn't sound like anyone could keep my attention. Then she said, "Kate you are an elegant, beautiful woman that is well-polished. You will find someone, I just know it. Don't give up."

"Yes," I agreed. "The next part of my life has to be better than the first part. It's my turn." Silently I thought about how lonely I was. So far, all that love had brought me was pain. It was easy for me to hide my feelings behind sarcasm and my playful sense of humor. To keep up the façade, I always spoke positive to others to portray that I had not lost my fire.

The only thing keeping me sane was Bikram Yoga. The hot yoga room was my safe place, where I could put my mat by "Darth Vader breather woman" or "70's mustache man," either of which kept me laughing. Yoga helped me keep a more positive attitude and helped me believe that my best days were still in front of me.

One evening the girls and I met for dinner and they immediately pushed me to tell them about more of my dating adventures. It's sad to say, but my friends were living through me and needed the stories. Speaking for them all, JoAnne said, "Come on, Kate. Fill us in on the latest gems of male humanity that you have met."

"Okay, you are going to love this one. I met a strikingly handsome man for lunch. We hit it off so he called me again. He seemed super together and is a custom builder in town. One night 'Bob the Builder' took me to a party at a hotel where there was a DJ and everyone was dancing. The music was loud and Bob was a good dancer, so I was actually having a good time. After we danced awhile, we sat down to have a drink when a couple came up and asked if they could sit with us. Bob invited them to join us for a drink.

"At this point the other man asked how long we've been in the 'lifestyle,' to which I said 'what do you mean?' He looked at his wife and then back at me and said, 'You don't know where you are, do you?' I told him that I obviously did not, so he went on to tell me that this was a swinger's party. My jaw nearly hit the floor! I turned to Bob who said to the man, 'She's vanilla.' Then Bob told me that being vanilla meant that I had not participated in the swinger life-style before."

Maggie said, "What did you do?"

"I said it was alright, that there was no pressure. I had a few more drinks and we danced some more, but I never went out with Bob again. I was not into casual sex much less swapping partners! I was just searching and trying to meet someone new but this was creating tension and I made it clear to myself that I was not giving up. I was tired of being alone. It is a wacko scene out there. You gals have been married so long you don't have a clue what it's like. A lot has changed since we dated. I admit that I wanted to try some new things, but being a swinger had never come to mind."

The girls raised their wine glasses and we had a toast. It was fun to trash the last year of my dates. Belinda said she thanked God it was not her as she would have freaked out.

I told the girls that "after everything that has happened to me I get a life pass. Nothing fazes me anymore."

Suddenly JoAnne piped up, "Alright. Who is going to tell her?"

Belinda said, "JoAnne, we said not tonight."

"What are you talking about?" I asked.

"Jax is going to have an exhibit at Bele Chere. He won an award for his photography!" JoAnne said. I interrupted and said, "I know. It was for his photos documenting war-torn Syria."

"So you already knew?" asked Maggie.

"About the award yes, but not his exhibit at Bele Chere" I replied.

Belinda said, "I don't think you ever forget your first love."

I was feeling flush from the news about Jax, so I quickly excused myself and said that I needed to go. It was true because I had Emma that weekend and wanted to stop by the grocery before getting her. After I left, JoAnne told the girls that Jax was off limits, and that he was not a topic I was willing to discuss.

When Emma and I arrived home I fixed our favorite dinner, "chicken with goop." It was chicken, Swiss cheese and cream of chicken soup. Comfort food is what this Mommy called it. Then we made popcorn and snuggled up together on the couch to watch the movie, "Hairspray." Spending quiet time with Emma helped me relax and I was able to let down my guard. She was getting accustomed to the visitation schedule and enjoyed being at her dad's house as well as mine. David was nice to her though he referred to me as "the starter wife." I hated that.

I would have preferred that Ken not marry me and use me to produce a child. As I always said: "You can't help who you love." I thought about Ken during the movie.

I remembered noticing Ken sitting all alone while I was at one of Emma's soccer games last week. Suddenly, it dawned on me that he had to miss me! He had to miss the couples we were friends with and the sense of family that I instilled into every holiday, every weekend, and every dinner. Then I realized that Ken had lost more than I did. He lost me.

Suddenly I felt bathed in satisfaction. I did everything for him. I was the funny one, the ice-breaker, the buffer. I opened every door by making it comfortable for people to be around him. They assumed he was straight and that he wanted a wife. In our crowd that was who he needed to be so I completed his image, but then he lost that. I realized that it must have become extremely lonely for Ken and that he must miss the life we once had. For many years he was like a best friend. He was easy to talk with and shop with. We had some good times and had some fun with our couple friends. Replacing long term friendships is very difficult and Ken may never find that again. I still had my girlfriends and Jill and mom.

I miss the time before I knew Ken was gay, before I knew he was indifferent to women. I miss the fantasy man that I dated. I lost nothing however, except a man who never loved me. That was a blessing because there was still a chance for me. I didn't want revenge; I just wanted to get busy living my life. I did love Ken. He is the father of my child and that is a bond which no one can ever break. I was just lonely longing to be loved and wanted to fill that empty void that was gnawing at me. I really enjoyed being married and I wanted to be someone's wife. I hated living alone.

I put this on my bathroom mirror with tape so I could see it every day.

There is no duty we so much underrate as the duty of being happy.
-Robert Louis Stevenson

Before I knew it, the weekend of Bele Chere arrived. Bele Chere attracts about 300,000 people a year to the three day music festival. It was a unique opportunity to see, taste, and hear some of the region's finest art, cuisine and music. Jill and Travis wanted us all to go to the street festival so we could watch the people, listen to the music and cut loose. I wanted to dance rock& roll music and have a glass of wine. Travis wanted to hear the country music he was a fan of guitar playing and Jill wanted to sing back up for any song she knew. She was so much fun to go out with.

Asheville's Bele Chere is the largest outdoor festival in the Southeast. During that weekend, most everyone is in good spirits, much like Mardi Gras in New Orleans. You can expect to see guys tanked on Jager and the streets full of dancing as the bars and street crowds blur together.

That year, Bele Chere was a party full of people dressed in funny clothes and so packed it was hard to move around. Street musicians playing their instruments and balloon artists creating hats and animals were all around us. We saw a table set up for whiskey pong and the wine bar was serving a special shooter called "Hellacious Death Drink," which we avoided. Instead, Jill ordered red wine for herself and for me and a beer for Travis. Then she noticed a large table of men and said to me, "Now Kate, there is a table full of men that you need to be looking at."

Travis motioned for our neighbors to join us and then told the bartender to put their drinks on his tab. The bartender never let our wine goblets get empty so Jill and I never really knew how much wine we were drinking.

By this time, Jill was getting tipsy and started giving marital advice to a couple nearby. It was their anniversary and the couple was celebrating and having a good time. Jill was so happy she started kissing on Travis. This was a haven for music lovers with plenty of live music and jamming taking place all around. I was having a good time chatting it up with the neighbor's when Jill said, "Kate go over there and talk to that big table of guys. I double-dog dare you."

Clearly Jill was not going to let this pass, so I marched right over to the table and announced, "I am single and my sister dared me to come over here." One of the men said, "Well... This is probably not the best table for you. Every year we meet at Bele Chere... and we're all gay." I ran over and grabbed Jill by the arm and brought her over to their table. I introduced her and then made the guy tell her the same thing he had told me. Then Jill started laughing and we hugged. "Only at Bele Chere!" she said.

We decided to go outside and walked around for a while. Then we stopped and listened to an Indie band and after that went back inside the bar. Once inside, Travis ran into a golfing buddy and they started swapping stories with each other.

One of the other bar patrons said, "I believe in aliens and find it all very interesting." To which Jill quipped, "Well, it won't be very interesting when you're burning in hell." Obviously, Jill was pleasantly intoxicated. Meanwhile, our wine glasses were still being refilled. The bar was full of people having a good time, and the vibrant nightlife scene was fascinating after dark. There was nothing to compare to this festival and the feeling of celebration in the air.

After a while, I looked over and saw that Jill was on the phone. When I pointed out to her that Travis was just across the room she said she was calling the Hotel Indigo looking for Jax. I told her, "No, you're not! I am sure his wife won't like that." Jill slurred, "I left him a message." I told her that she was drunk.

The song "All the Single Ladies" was playing so I convinced Jill to let me teach her a few dance moves that Emma had taught me. Jill is such a terrible dancer; I was bent over laughing. The harder she tried the worse it got. I was really feeling good and loved being with my big sister.

Jill left the dance floor and motioned to me to come and sit with her at the bar. We struck up a conversation with our neighbor, Dan, and his wife. Dan was a funny guy and was telling a joke when Jill saw Jax walk in. Suddenly she jumped up and pushed her way through the crowd to get to him. Travis looked over and saw Jill yelling at Jax and then she began to beat on his chest and swing at him. Travis ran over and asked her what she was doing. Belligerently, Jill said, "This son of a gun just told me he has been divorced for a year."

"So why are you hitting him?" Travis asked. Jill screamed over the crowd, "Because Kate still loves him, she always has."

"It is such a privilege to watch your mind at work" Travis said as he lovingly took Jill by the waist and guided her over to the dance floor.

"Kate." Hearing my name, I looked around and saw Jax. Slowly he walked toward me, flashing that grin that I always loved. I hugged his neck and said, "I have been looking for you."

"Nugget, my feelings for you have never changed" Jax said. "You are the only one I have ever wanted and I will never leave you again."

I put my hands on his face as he kissed me deeply, holding me tight. "Jax" I said. "I have loved you a long time. You are the love of my life."

One embrace and one kiss on a crowded dance floor in a noisy bar during Bele Chere. Finally, after all those years, my life started to feel right.

T. T. Johnson is available for speaking engagements and public appearances. For more information contact:

T.T. Johnson
C/O Advantage Books
P.O. Box 160847
Altamonte Springs, FL 32716

info@ advbooks.com

To purchase additional copies of this book or other books published by Advantage Books call our order number at:

407-788-3110 (Book Orders Only)

or visit our bookstore website at:
www.advbookstore.com

Longwood, Florida, USA
"we bring dreams to life"™
www.advbookstore.com

CPSIA information can be obtained at www.ICGtesting.com
Printed in the USA
LVOW05s1650230214

374817LV00001B/1/P